DO-OVER LOVE & MURDER

A LOVE & MURDER NOVEL

EDIE RAMER

Blue Walrus Books

Paperback ISBN: 978-1-939328-36-6

Created with Vellum

ABOUT DO-OVER LOVE & MURDER

Hailey is the careful one. The sensible one. And now she's the one in trouble – about to go into the Witness Protection Program.

When Hailey does something, she does it properly. So when she picks the wrong man to have an affair with, he's really wrong. Organized crime wrong. Now she, her mom, and her baby are adjusting to life in the small town of Trouble Bay, Wisconsin, where the streets are quiet in winter and loud with tourists in the summer. Not a place where the mafia would think to look for her. She feels safe, but someone took her control away once, and she's not going to let it happen again.

And then there's the man next door and their disturbing first encounter…

Wounded physically and emotionally, US Army Sergeant Wes Hard-

ing fights to attain peace of mind, which might be the best – or the least – that he can hope for.

Soon after Wes loses half of his left leg in a botched military mission, he loses his fiancée, who can't live with his injuries. He tells himself he's lucky to have a therapy dog and a prosthetic leg. His uncle, too, who insists that Wes stay in his home in the town of Trouble Bay, Wisconsin.

Wes suspects his new neighbor isn't telling the truth about where she came from. He's getting his own life together, and he's not about to intrude on hers. But she's impossible to avoid and more impossible to ignore. He knows she has secrets, and he wonders how dangerous they may be…

This is a new life for both Hailey and Wes. Anything can happen – for the good or the bad.

1

MIAMI: JUNE

THE HOUSEKEEPER USHERED Hailey into the living room of Leo's south Miami penthouse, or—as Hailey thought of it now—the scene of the crime and the last place she wanted to be.

Despite the Miami heat, the vast white-and-gray living room gave her chills. She stepped up to the wall of windows and gazed down at the ocean meeting the sky. Beautiful, but she was too tired to appreciate the view. Since she'd found out the test results last week, she hadn't slept well, and she was wobbling on her feet. Maybe once she told Leo why she needed to talk to him, she could sleep like—

"You're here." Leo's voice was thick with emotion.

Taking a deep breath, Hailey turned to see him striding toward her, a big man with dark hair and matching eyes. She held out her hands to stop him from embracing her.

This was so wrong. Her life was beginning to feel like a soap opera, and she was the last woman anyone would expect to be in this situation.

Which proved that even the most sensible woman could do stupid things when a man was involved.

"Don't. Please. I'm here because I have something to tell you."

Leo stopped two feet away, but his eyes burned into hers. As if he knew why she was here, which was ridiculous.

"Then we'll talk." He moved to the couch and patted the seat next to him. "Sit."

The *sit* command sounded like he was talking to a dog, and she took the cream-colored leather chair across from him. His dark eyes lit up, as if he took her reluctance as a challenge. An obstacle he planned to overcome.

Looking at this tall, muscular man, she wondered what she'd been thinking of by dating him. But the real mystery was why he'd pursued her. He was a multimillionaire who bought and sold stocks like she bought and sold ... well, not much, because she was notoriously careful with her money.

Leo was out of her league. She didn't feel a twinge admitting it, because it was a league she didn't care to join. Her time with him had been a fling. It had taken her two months to realize she'd rather stay home and read a good book than spend an evening listening to him talking about his great stock choices, the celebrities he knew, and the golf games that he always seemed to win.

"You've come back to me." He leaned forward, his eyes brighter, demanding her attention.

She frowned, wondering for what must be the thousandth time why he was fixated on her. Stinking-wealthy men like him could have their pick of beautiful women.

She wasn't modest. She knew she was attractive. Not gorgeous or stunning, but pretty in an understated way. Instead of fiery and hot, like Leo, she was cool and reserved. Not a woman whom a man would carry on his sleeve the way wealthy women wore diamonds and the latest fashions. Anything that shouted to the world: *Look at me! Look how important and rich and fabulous I am!*

Maybe she reminded him of the auburn-haired wife who was divorcing him. Because, of course the first thing Hailey had done after giving him her phone number was to check him out online. She'd even seen a photo of his wife that had stopped her breath for a long moment. Polina Vasnev, a daughter of a former Russian diplomat, was a brighter, vibrant version of her.

When Leo had met Hailey at her favorite South Beach restaurant, he'd told her he had a penchant for redheads. He'd even mentioned his divorce, telling her their lawyers were fighting over who should get what. She understood that. Where there was wealth, there were people fighting to get the biggest shares. Though his marriage situation had bothered her, in the end she'd stopped seeing him because she just didn't like him that much.

He'd pleaded with her to stay, but she'd walked away, feeling a huge sense of relief. Every single woman she knew would probably think she was insane, but she'd sensed that she'd jumped out of the path of a train heading straight toward her.

Only the train hadn't missed her after all. Now, nearly two months later, she carried the proof of their short relationship inside her.

Like millions of women before her who'd been in a similar situation, she was wondering why her birth control hadn't worked.

She thought that some people would say it was meant to be.

She wasn't one of them.

Facing him, she took a deep breath, then blurted, "I'm pregnant."

He sat still, not one muscle moving, his eyes bright, radiating triumph. Almost as if he'd been waiting for her to say that, which was ridiculous. They hadn't had sex the first three weeks. When they had, she'd been taking birth control pills *and* she'd insisted that he use a condom.

Three weeks later, she'd missed her period.

She *never* missed her period. Ever.

She'd waited a week, hoping it would come soon.

Then another week.

And another.

She was twenty-six and, oh, God, she just didn't want to be pregnant with Leo's baby.

When the seventh week had come and gone, she'd stopped off at the drugstore and bought three different pregnancy tests. She'd prayed, but as many other women had found out before her, her prayers were weak, and his sperm was strong. All three tests had affirmed her pregnancy.

The next week, so had her gynecologist.

So here she was, staring at a man she wished now that she'd never met.

"It's *my* baby," he said, his voice rough.

She nodded.

"You swear?" He pushed off his chair and took long strides toward her, his eyes drilled into hers. "You swear on the baby's life?"

She frowned. *Swear on the baby's life*? Who said things like that? "It's yours. I don't need to swear on anything. I haven't slept with anyone else since we dated."

"Yes!" he said. "Yes!"

Then he reached down, his hands on both her shoulders, drew her up to her feet and kissed her hard, his teeth digging into her lips.

"Woohoo!" he shouted, lifting her so her head was above his, his hands gripping her upper arms too tightly as he grinned triumphantly.

"You're hurting me." She squirmed.

He lowered her, his eyes glittering. "I'll take care of you. I'll take care of all the expenses. I'll find the best doctor. You'll stay here, and I'll make sure you eat the right foods."

"Excuse me?" She was getting a bad feeling about this. "I have insurance. I don't need your money or your advice on what to eat. I don't need your help. Of course, once the baby is born, I expect you to pay support, but I'm not giving up my life for you. I don't need a man to control me."

He straightened his spine. "You're having *my* baby."

"And you're still married."

"Argh." He put his hands on each side of his head and exhaled again, reminding her of a frustrated grizzly. "The baby needs a father. A woman is not enough."

She crossed her arms under her breasts, wishing that while he'd held her above the floor, she'd taken advantage of the position and kicked him in his tender place. "I was raised by a single mother. My father was always there for me, but he didn't live with us, and she did most of the hard work. I think she's done a damn good job."

He made a growling sound low in his throat. Then he sucked in his breath and nodded. "Perhaps I said that wrong."

Perhaps? She stared at him, not blinking, not saying anything.

"You're right. I understand. You don't need me, but I need you. I need the baby." He held his hands out in a pleading motion. "You and the baby will make my life complete. I don't want to control you. I just want to make sure both of you have the best doctors in Miami."

She narrowed her eyes at him, then felt a great yawn overtaking her. *Oh, no. Not this. Not now.* She'd read about this. Pregnancy tiredness in the first trimester. Add that to her lack of sleep—and the relief that she had finally told Leo about the pregnancy—and she felt like she could curl up on a wooden floor and start snoring.

She swallowed the yawn, her chin jutting up. "That sounds like the definition of control to me."

"It's not control. It's caring."

Another yawn overtook her, this one stronger. She put her hand over her mouth but couldn't hide it.

"You're tired," he said. "You need a nap."

"I'll be fine."

"You're not fine. You need to take a nap."

Another yawn started. She put her hand over her mouth again, but now her eyelids wanted to close.

"I'll take you to the guest room. I won't bother you." He put his hand over his heart. "You have my word."

"I'm fine. I'll just go home and—"

"You are *not* fine. When was the last time you slept through the night?"

She counted in her head. Two weeks? Or was it longer? Of course, she'd slept during the two weeks, though not through the nights. And during the days, she'd worked. Going through life as if nothing had changed, when, in reality, her life was turning upside down.

And now the sleepiness had caught up to her and was sapping her energy. She reluctantly nodded. "Just for a short time."

He put his hand over her back, as if she were fragile, and she allowed him to escort her to the guest bedroom. She didn't want to argue now. Not with another strong wave of tiredness clogging her brain. She needed to be at her sharpest when she asserted her independence.

Leo was too suffocating. Too bossy. Already trying to take her over.

At least he wasn't taking her to his bedroom. He probably knew she wouldn't allow that. That she could walk right out of his life as easily as she'd walked into his penthouse tonight.

The baby was growing inside her body. Right now, it was up to her to make the decisions that were best for both of them.

She'd tell him that when she wasn't so tired.

It did seem that he genuinely wanted the baby. But how odd was that? Most men who were in the middle of a divorce wanted anything but a baby.

She wanted to trust him, but doubts niggled inside her, and she didn't know why.

He ushered her into the bedroom. She kicked off her shoes and lay down on the bed and closed her eyes. Feeling his stare on her, she muttered, "Go away."

He chuckled. A second later, she heard the door click shut. She opened her eyes to make sure he'd left, then she closed them again. "Good," she whispered. "Good..."

2

Hailey woke up with a start. She instantly knew where she was—a guest bedroom in Leo's penthouse. Ugh. She'd wanted this to be an in-and-out kind of a thing. *Just letting you know you'll be a father... I don't want you in my life anymore, but I felt obligated to tell you.*

She grabbed her purse from the nightstand, then checked the time on her cell phone. She'd only slept about ten minutes, but she felt better. And why not? After all, short naps worked for cats.

Getting out of bed, she finger-combed her strawberry-colored hair, then straightened her top and shorts. They fit her now, but in another month or two, she'd probably need bigger clothes.

Sighing, she rubbed the back of her neck. She had promised to visit her mother in the morning to help her with her computer.

"I have a problem," her mother had said.

Most likely it was her mother who had caused the problem. Men loved her redheaded mother, but she insisted that computers hated her.

Her mother's come-to-mama gene with men had missed Hailey, but Hailey did have her mother's long legs as well as the red hair.

She also had her mother's independent gene, because she wasn't ready to let a man tie her down and tell her what to do.

For a short time, she'd enjoyed Leo's machismo, but she'd never thought she loved him. Never thought he'd be her Mr. Forever. He was too overpowering. Too domineering. And she was a woman who didn't like being dominated.

These thoughts swirled through her mind as she picked up her purse and hurried to the door. Planning on sneaking out, she was glad that she'd worn her sandals with the rubber soles. When she reached the end of the wall that led to the living room and then to freedom, she stood for a moment, listening. She didn't want to run into Leo and have to argue with him. She'd told him about the baby, and now she just wanted to leave.

"Your father wants to talk to you. He's on your office phone."

Hailey recognized the clipped tone of Leo's assistant.

"I'm texting Polina," Leo said. "She'll be happy to hear my news."

"You want me to tell your father you can't talk to him because you're texting happy news to your wife?"

Hailey pressed against the wall of the front hallway. What news would Leo's wife be happy to hear? Not her pregnancy. That would be cruel.

Leo swore at his assistant, then said. "Okay, okay. I'll go."

She remained pressed against the wall as their footsteps trod toward his office in the back. When their footsteps faded, she released let her pent-up breath and tiptoed into the living room. She needed to cross it to get to the elevator. Nearing the glass coffee table, she spotted Leo's cell phone.

She paused, and a monologue started in her mind. *Oh, no. You are not going over there to read his texts. You are not doing anything so stupid. Just because the heroine in the whodunits always gets away with snooping, that doesn't mean you will.*

Her inner voice was right, yet she stood still instead of hurrying out of the penthouse. Perhaps it was the nap, but her brain seemed to be buzzing at full power. Too many things had bothered her about Leo's reaction to the pregnancy. Something felt off. Wrong. Why had Leo been so eager to call his wife right now? His *separated* wife? Maybe they had a sick relationship where they got their kicks from hurting each other.

He was the father of her child. If that was the kind of man he was, she needed to know.

Her mind made up, she strode to the couch. She would quickly scan the texts. It would take less than a minute, and she'd be long gone by the time Leo returned.

Like a heroine in a made-for-TV movie, she picked up the cell phone, and in a second, she was reading the first text.

My Madonna, don't worry about her. She's sleeping now.

Hailey stiffened. *Madonna*? That's what he called the wife who was in the process of divorcing him?

This made no sense.

The next sentence was from his wife.

Leo, if you really want to do this, be cautious. She might guess.

Hailey stared at the words. This wasn't a message she would type to a man she was in the process of divorcing.

Her gaze slid to Leo's next text.

Don't worry that she'll guess. She doesn't suspect a thing. She's got the baby in the oven, and when it comes out, it will be straight into my hands. And from mine into yours. The hands of my true love.

Hailey gripped the phone tightly, stopping her furious thoughts. She didn't have time for anger now. Right now she needed to read more texts.

In only seven months, the baby will pop out, right into my eager hands.

Eww. His first text said the baby would slide out into his hands. Now it was popping out into his hands. Not only was he a weird jerk, he was stuck on terrible metaphors.

And then into your hands, my beautiful wife.

I do want a baby, but—

It's the only way we can do this. No one will know it's not yours. Besides, it's done now. You agreed with me.

We should have kept on trying. I don't like this.

I can't wait too long. My father wants to make sure we have babies.

I would have been fine with an adoption.

Not an adoption. It has to be my baby.

I know. You told me. Men and their egos.

If my father knew the baby wasn't mine, he wouldn't want me to take over the business. Don't worry. Everything will work out. I'll convince her to go to your gynecologist. She's like warm butter in my hands. She melts whenever I look at her.

Leo, I'm not sure—

You have a soft heart, my darling. Don't fear. There will be an unfortunate death on the delivery table. I already talked to the doctor. It's all set up. Money has passed hands.

Leo? Leo? Where did you go? I suppose she's awoken. Why can't you just give her money? Pay her for the baby? I don't like the idea of killing the baby's mother. I don't like it at all.

AS COLD SEEPED into the marrow of Hailey's bones, she took pictures of the texts with her cell phone. Her first instinct had been to send them to her email, but then they would show up in his sent emails, and he could track them down. Not that she expected him to check his sent emails, but despite this one great screw-up, she was naturally cautious and meticulous. The opposite of Leo's heedless and volatile character.

As soon as she left Leo's place, she would head straight to her father's office. A respected lawyer, he would know what to do.

She had what she wanted—pictures of the most damning texts—but she was naturally thorough and went back a month in his texting history as she listened for footsteps, praying that Leo or his assistant would stay away until she had everything she needed.

The first few texts were innocuous, including two to her. Then she read one that seemed to be about money laundering, and another one about robbing tourists visiting the Red See—a private men's club his family apparently ran—by using tourists' credit card information.

Another text mentioned selling assault guns to criminals. Another one complained that an undocumented dancer from Russia had become pregnant, and when they forced her to get an abortion, she died.

They'd tossed the fetus and the dancer's body into the Atlantic Ocean.

Hailey took more pictures of the damning texts, ignoring her hands that kept wanting to shake.

Another text was about buying and selling assault rifles and machine guns. She took a picture of that, too, wondering how many crimes Leo, his father, and their associates were committing.

Apparently as many as they could get their hands on.

More texts had been sent to family and friends. Four were about her. He was adamant on going through with the plan to impregnate her, though his wife kept expressing her doubts.

Hailey cringed a little for his wife, who apparently had been a reluctant part of Leo's scheme. But in the end, his wife had buckled, so Hailey didn't feel too bad for her.

Finally, she saw that ten minutes had passed. Leo might return to the living room any moment. She thought of taking the phone with her and showing the phone numbers to her father, but removing it might corrupt the evidence. She replaced the cell phone on the coffee table. She'd been in this room too long. She needed to leave. Now.

Hurrying away, she felt sick and angry and scared.

She didn't know what was going to happen. She just knew it wasn't going to be easy. And it wasn't going to be pretty.

As the elevator doors silently slid shut behind her, she began to shake, her hands over her stomach, as if protecting the tiny being growing inside of her.

3

MIAMI: TWO WEEKS LATER

THE CHAUFFEURED CAR SLOWED. Polina had held in her anger and her anguish today. Her father-in-law had told her to shut up and not say anything when she'd talked to the police first and then the US Marshals. She had nodded to them all, her head lowered in obeisance, when what she had really wanted to do was to scream and cry and rage.

And in her father-in-law's case, kick him in the place he treasured so much.

She knew what Peter Vasnev was like. He'd even looked at her —his son's wife—as if she were another piece of ass.

Animal. Pig. Rutting pig.

Like father, like son.

Almost. She knew Leo loved her.

But he loved himself more.

And his love hadn't stopped him from sleeping with other women.

Her heart ached. She had never agreed with Leo's plan. She'd begged him to wait, but it was like talking to a spoiled child. What he wanted, he wanted *right now*. Not later.

She blamed Leo's mother as well as his father. Olga treated Leo like a little king and, at the same time, was critical of him. Now Polina realized that perhaps he deserved his mother's criticism. Perhaps without it, Leo would have been as cold and cruel as his father. A man who stuck his dick into any woman who would open her legs for him. And when a man was a multibillionaire and the head of Miami's Russian Mafia, there were a lot of women with open legs.

The thought sickened her.

The car stopped in front of her home overlooking the ocean and, before she could say good-bye, her father-in-law hugged her.

She turned her head so he could only kiss her cheek, then pushed away as the driver opened the door. "Good-bye," she said. Her back stiff, she hopped out and marched away, into the house, up the stairway.

Her chef was around somewhere, but she didn't call for him. Instead she ran to her suite, started the bath, shed her clothes, then hopped into the tub. Warm water whirled around her, and she leaned back, her eyes closed as tears traveled down her cheeks. Not tears of helplessness or surrender. Tears of anger.

Her life was crumbling into tiny pieces.

If only Leo had been more patient. Her doctor had said her menstrual cycle was short, but that didn't mean she couldn't have babies. She could still get pregnant. It just might take longer.

Leo hadn't wanted to take that chance. Not since his father had a new mistress who was about the same age as Polina. The new mistress already had a healthy son, three years old. She was fertile.

Polina knew that Leo's father was supporting two daughters from two other women, but they didn't worry Leo.

What worried him was that his father's next child might be male.

He wouldn't wait for Polina to get pregnant.

Damn him for doing this. Damn him for not waiting. Damn him for caring more about what his father might do than how she felt about this.

Damn him, damn him, damn him.

As much as she had loved him, right now she hated him. Her life was falling apart, and there wasn't anything she could do to stop it.

Her father-in-law's team of lawyers was representing her and Leo. They'd promised to save Polina from serving time, but they hadn't made the same promises for Leo.

And the same two questions kept hammering in her brain: Why hadn't she been stronger? Why hadn't she left him?

Shivering, she stepped out of the tub, then crumpled onto her knees on the marble-tiled bathroom floor. She sobbed, horrible cries that sounded as if her soul was ripping apart.

With all Leo's faults, she'd loved him.

But now...

She lifted her head, her teeth gritted and her fists clenched.

She hated Leo.

She hated his father.

She hated his mother.

She hated the woman who carried Leo's child, though she knew that was wrong.

And, most of all, she hated herself because of what she planned to do. The baby's mother had told Leo that she hadn't wanted the baby.

Polina wanted a baby. Wanted it more than anything.

What if Leo was right, and she would never be able to have a baby? To pop one out? Ever?

Polina grabbed the towel and patted her body dry. Right now, Hailey was holed up somewhere, waiting to testify, the Feds watching over her.

The trial would take awhile. Longer than usual, with so many incriminating texts that Leo had sent to different people for different crimes. If the texts had been only about the baby, he probably would remain free until the trial, but because of his other texts, the Feds had labeled him as a flight risk and were keeping him locked up until after the trial.

The lawyers had promised Leo's father that he wouldn't be charged with anything, despite Leo's texts. But they couldn't say the same to Leo.

An ache filled her, and she didn't know if the ache was for her empty womb, her empty bed, her empty life, or even her empty heart.

Leo would have prison time. She didn't know how long. She had no choice but to wait. Not patiently. Angrily. Sorrowfully.

And when this trial was over, she wasn't sure how she would feel. Wasn't sure what she would do. It might be something good. Or something bad. Or something crazy.

4

Trouble Bay, Wisconsin: July

Wes Harding stood in the driveway and stared at the blue ranch home that was probably close to fifty years old, located on the block behind Main Street. It appeared to be in decent condition, though the blue paint was faded by the sun and the years. Next to Wes, his service dog, Spock, a black lab, stared at the house, too, his mouth open in a happy smile. Probably glad to get out of the car and have a long pee on the grass.

"This is your home." Wes turned left to his uncle Blake, looking up a couple of inches. When Wes was a kid, he and his mother used to drive from Milwaukee to Trouble Bay in the Door County peninsula of Wisconsin every summer to visit his uncle who'd reminded Wes of a superhero. "I'm not kicking you out of your own house."

"I live in a cabin."

"Bullshit."

"No bull. I bought a cabin with a view of Lake Michigan." His tall, lanky uncle grinned. "Not because of you. It's the women."

"The women?"

His uncle's grin widened. "I had to move farther away. Every day at least one or more would stop by and ask me to fix something."

"Yeah? And what did they offer to give you in return?"

"Not money." His uncle winked. "Just dinner and conversation."

Wes laughed, the sound genuine for the first time in months. He could see why the women would be after his uncle. He was a year younger than his mom, which made him about fifty-six, and he still looked like a superhero, though his brown hair was mixed with gray now and there were lines on his face. He'd married twice, but neither marriage had lasted. His mom had said that his uncle had bad taste in women.

Bad taste in women was something Wes understood too well.

"Be careful," Uncle Blake said. "Their single daughters will be after you now."

Wes stopped laughing, and he gestured at the house. "Lead the way."

Blake strode forward, Wes stepping carefully behind him. By now, he was proficient at walking with his below-the-knee prosthetic leg. He counted himself lucky to have gotten a service dog so quickly, especially a great dog like Spock.

Still, he didn't blame his former fiancée for breaking up with him. He'd been a mess, physically and emotionally. He'd seen the horror on her face when she visited him in the hospital. The sick look that said *I didn't sign up for this.*

She was better off without him. And he was better off without her, because he'd felt nothing when she'd run from his room, sobbing. As if she were a stranger, someone he'd never cared about.

Stepping inside the house, he pushed away the memories of

Renee as his uncle showed him around the three-bedroom, two-bathroom house.

"I've got a surprise for you." Blake continued down the hall and turned into the smaller bedroom.

Wes smelled a faint paint odor as he followed Blake. The room was the same pale blue color he remembered from when he was a kid, staying overnight. Blake didn't stop as he headed for the closet and slid open the door.

Instead of hangers or even a few old clothes, there was a washer and dryer, one stacked over the other.

Wes looked at his uncle. "You did this for me?"

"Hey, it's good for me, too." Blake slapped him on the back. "I was lucky to get out of my army tours uninjured, at least physically. War isn't for sissies."

For the second time since he'd woken up in the hospital bed with his left leg below his knee gone and the doctors telling him he was lucky to have that knee, tears heated Wes's eyes.

He blinked them back.

"Thank you," he said, his voice ragged. "Thank you."

He remembered what his mother used to say when things got tough. When her hours were cut. When his father was late with his support money. When her car wouldn't work.

We'll get through this, sweetie. You and I, we're so lucky to have each other. And God, too. She's watching over us.

He looked out the window, but all he saw was the white ranch next door.

"What are you thinking?" his uncle asked.

"Mom."

"Yeah." There was a moment of silence. Then Blake said, "She died too young."

"I miss her. For a while, I thought I'd be the one who might not make it. Instead she died. Fucking cancer."

"That was a tough time."

"Did you know that every morning of every day until I joined the army, she would tell me she loved me, and that she and God were glad I was born?"

"Sounds like her." Blake's rough voice thickened. "I'm not the optimist that your mom was, but in this case, I think maybe she's right."

"She loved you, too."

"She was the best. I never had a son or a daughter, but I think of you as a son."

Wes nodded his thanks. He'd had two people in the world now who loved him. Three if he believed his father, who'd visited him in the hospital before flying back home to his wife and Wes's half brother in Indiana, who Wes had never been invited to meet.

He'd learned long ago not to expect anything from his dad and had been surprised to see him at the hospital. Renee, too, who'd cried over him, saying she was sorry. Wanting forgiveness, which he gave her just so she could leave.

He hadn't heard from either of them since.

He shoved down the bad thoughts and focused on the good things in his life.

His uncle.

His prosthetic leg.

His service dog.

A house to live in.

The best mother ever. Maybe she wasn't here in person, but in his mind, he could still see her and hear her. As if she were in heaven, smiling down at him.

And he was alive while so many others weren't. Shouldn't he make the best of his life? Try to enjoy the day? The hour? The minute?

"You know what else Mom would tell me? That I could do anything I put my mind to."

"She told me that a few times, too." One side of Blake's mouth lifted in a half smile. "A few thousand. So, what is it you want to do?"

"I don't have that figured out yet." Wes shrugged. "There's nothing wrong with my hands or my mind. You're making furniture. I'm not sure if that's for me, but there could be a great satisfaction in creating something that you're proud of."

"That's it? I thought you were going to say that you wanted a woman." Blake frowned. "Are you still thinking about the girl who ditched you? She wasn't a keeper. You're better off without her."

"I'm not thinking about her or any woman. Not yet. I'm just finding my place in life."

"You better watch what you say. Especially when you're talking about a woman. Whenever I say I'm not ready for something, whatever I don't want always seems to strike me in the head like a lightning bolt coming down from a stormy sky."

"That's not going to happen to me." Wes turned and pointed out the window ... just in time to realize the sunny skies had turned gray and thunder rumbled, followed by a lightning strike that shook the ground.

His uncle laughed, and Wes stared at the window, shaking his head. This meant nothing to him. Lightning would strike him before love. Right now, he needed to concentrate on living and walking and starting a new life.

He had no room for love. No time for love. And even if he did, his heart was too numb for love.

5

Trouble Bay: April

US Marshal Tracey Milhouse, a big-boned woman in her early forties wearing black slacks and a long-sleeved white blouse, pulled two suitcases out of the SUV, then rolled them to the sidewalk.

Holding her sleeping baby in her arms, Hayley knew she should offer to help Tracey, but like her mother, she was too busy staring at the ranch house on this quiet street in the block behind the main road of this small town.

None of it felt real to her. This place—this town—reminded her of an old movie set. Tracey had told them the fifty-year-old L-shaped ranch was fifteen hundred square feet. Inside, it had a kitchen, living room, three bedrooms, and two full bathrooms.

She hadn't mentioned the big window in the front or the flowering crab apple tree with the pink flower petals open. The exterior was Lannon stone on the bottom and white paneling above. There was a driveway and a two-car attached garage, with a tall evergreen tree in the front yard.

Hayley told herself that she should feel grateful for the temporary home and the new start. Grateful that she could use her real first name, only changing the spelling. But she'd lived in apartments and condos her entire life, so this house was a huge change.

More than that, she was used to living in a bustling, always alive city. Always something to see or do, night or day.

This town, with a thousand inhabitants in the winter, felt sleepy, with only the sound of an occasional car or truck driving down the main street a block behind them, plus a few bird chirps and dog barks. The silences between these sounds gave Hayley goose bumps, and not the good kind. She didn't feel as if she were in a different part of the US. She felt as if she were in a different universe.

Tracey had told them the population multiplied to ten times a thousand in the summer months, and the tourists should start trickling into the town in a few weeks. Hayley rocked the baby in her arms. Maybe when it wasn't so quiet she would feel more normal.

For now, though, she needed to be grateful that she'd read the incriminating texts on Leo's cell phone. Grateful that she was alive. Grateful to hold her baby in her arms. Grateful that her mother had insisted on coming with her, leaving behind her brightly decorated condo, her many friends, and her thriving real estate business.

Hayley had left her dad behind. That had been hard. Two hours after she had fled Leo's penthouse, her father had canceled all of his appointments, then had driven her and her mother to the US Marshals Service in Miami. He'd insisted that the marshals transfer their assets to their new names and that they add the social security income they'd accrued to the new name.

She would miss seeing her dad every couple weeks or so. As a child, she'd mostly lived with her mother, and her father was busy with his law practice and his second wife, who was also a lawyer. But he'd always made time for Hayley. And he'd always been there when she needed him.

"You okay?" Susan asked.

"I have to be okay," she said.

"So you should." Tracey gave her a pointed stare. "If you hadn't snapped pictures of the cell phone texts, your baby would be in Polina Vasnev's arms instead of yours."

"Snooping has always been underrated." Susan slid her arm around Hayley's shoulders. "I'm counting my blessings. And just think of the new skills we'll learn."

"Grass mowing," Hayley said. They both laughed, though her laughter wasn't as strong as her mother's.

"Mowing's easy," Tracey said. "In winter, you'll be shoveling the sidewalk and the driveway."

Hayley and Susan stared at each other, wide-eyed, then Susan turned to Tracey. "I suppose that's good exercise."

Tracey cackled with laughter and slapped Susan's back. "I like your attitude. You could pay someone to plow your driveway. That's what I do. You can even pay someone to shovel the side-walk, though it really is good exercise, and not as bad as shoveling the whole driveway. Come on, I'll take you inside for the tour."

Hayley and Susan each grabbed a suitcase, then followed Tracey into the furnished house. Holding Finn against her chest and dragging the wheeled suitcase behind her, Hayley was too numb to care what the interior looked like, but her mom took one glance at the oversized furniture and beige carpet in the front room and made a face.

"Eww." Susan sniffed at the couch, two matching recliners, and a television mounted on the wall. "The TV is barely thirty-six inches. The dirt-brown recliners are ugly, and ugly is never fine. A man must've picked out the furniture. No woman would have such bad taste."

In the kitchen, her mother's tone changed slightly. She liked the porcelain-tiled floor and the U-shaped quartz counter with a small island, but she despised the fake wood tabletop. She sniffed at the out-of-date cupboards but said they would do. When she opened the cupboards, she stared at the dinner plates, a horrified look on her face, putting her hand over her heart.

"They're not the best," Tracey said, "but they came with the rental."

"I would rather eat on paper plates." Susan closed the cupboard door, then looked at Hayley. "Don't worry, honey. I'll go shopping and buy something much nicer."

Hayley nodded. She was tired and wanted to settle in and didn't care that much about the plates. Not right now, anyway. But she knew better than to tell that to her mother.

"At least it has a side door." She gestured at the hallway a few feet from the counter.

"There are hooks for jackets or coats," Tracey said, "and a rubber mat for shoes or boots."

"Boots," Susan repeated and shivered.

She and Hayley walked to the hallway. "There's a basement!" Susan said, peering downward.

"The washing machine and dryer are down there," Tracey said. "I wanted to get you a newer house, but this was the best I could get. The house is a nice size. Bigger than either of your places."

"You're right." Susan sighed. "It's about twice as big as mine. I'm just being a grouch. Don't worry. I can fix this up."

"Here are your cars." Tracey opened the door at the end of the hall and stepped back to let them peek inside. "They're the same years as your cars." Tracey turned to Hayley. "I suggested an SUV because of the baby, but the sedan is similar to your old car, and it actually costs a bit more. And the mileage is close to what you had."

"Hayley's dad insisted on it." Susan's eyes brightened with humor. "Didn't he?"

"I believe that's correct," Tracey said.

Susan laughed, but Hayley had a hard time dredging up a smile. She was too tired to care about the size of the car or the mileage. Whatever it was would do. Her life had been turned upside down. For months she'd been in protective custody, along with her mother, and then her baby. Now she just wanted to sleep for as long as Finn let her sleep.

"You're okay?" her mom asked.

"I'm lucky." She blurted the words out. "I have you, and I have Finn, and we're *alive.*"

Her mother's eyes dampened, and she stepped forward and put her arms around her, Finn between them. They stayed like that for a moment, then Finn squirmed and cried out.

Her mom stepped back, and Hayley looked at Tracey, who was beaming at them.

"I'll show you the baby's room." Tracey headed out to the hallway and through the kitchen.

She'd told them earlier that the house had three bedrooms and two bathrooms. Hayley's bedroom was the biggest, with a full-sized bed and a bassinet, which she'd insisted upon. The smallest was already set up for the baby, though the crib and the set of drawers were not the best. Hayley looked at her mother, who was frowning. She was probably already planning on how to spruce it up.

Hayley winced, feeling guilty for dragging her into this. In Miami, her mother had men and women friends and was usually laughing and busy. She loved to dance and didn't care if she sang off-key. She'd once told Hayley that she liked to treat every day as if it were a dessert. But now—thanks to Hayley's bad taste in men—every day was going to be a side dish along with a dried-up piece of meat.

"I know it's sleepy and quiet here," Tracey said. "That's part of the reason we thought of Trouble Bay. No one would expect you to live in a small town. And once you get used to it, you'll be surprised at the way the townspeople look after each other."

"I don't want to be looked after," Hayley said, then yawned, unable to cover her mouth while she held the baby.

Tracey gave her a sympathetic look. "You look like you could roll into bed and sleep for a week."

"I wish, but Finn's sleeping schedule and mine don't seem to match." She barely had the words out when Finn made a chirping sound.

She stood still for a moment, and the other two women didn't speak. Hayley wasn't even sure they breathed. Then Finn sagged against her breast.

Susan and Tracey laughed softly. Hayley rocked Finn as Tracey and her mother talked. Hayley's eyelids wanted to shut, and she forced herself to keep them open.

"You're falling asleep," Tracey said finally. "Is there anything else you need now?"

Hailey and Susan shook their heads. Tracey gave Susan two sets of keys, then told them to call if they had any questions and promised she'd check in with them soon.

They walked her to the front door and watched her hurry to her car. Her mother closed the door, then turned.

"Our new life is beginning right now."

Before Hayley could reply, the baby whimpered once. Then came a sob, followed by a louder sob.

Hayley rocked him again. She was tired, in a strange place, and her baby was hungry and crabby.

So was she, with *sleepy* added to the list.

She turned into the living room and glanced out the big front window. "I need to sit down."

"I'll get the blinds," Susan said just as Finn went from a whimper to a full-blown cry.

As her mother slanted the blinds so no one could see Hayley breastfeeding, Hayley plopped down on the faux suede recliner. In seconds, Finn's mouth clamped onto her breast, his howls stopped.

The silence was wonderful. Hayley sighed as her mother hurried into the kitchen, then returned with a dish towel that she draped over Hayley's shoulder.

"You know what I've just discovered?" Hayley asked.

Her mother shook her head.

"This chair is freaking comfortable."

Her mother laughed, loud and long, her knees bent, her hand over her belly. When her laughing turned to chuckles, she sat on the matching recliner, then pressed the lever that raised the footrest. As the baby suckled, her mother breathed out, "*Aaah.*"

They both remained silent, the baby's small noises the only sound until his sucking slowed and then stopped. Hayley burped him but still didn't get up. "This might not be so bad."

"I'm going to make this place beautiful," her mother said, her voice dreamy.

"We'll have a great life here."

"And I'm going to learn how to shoot a gun."

Hayley sat straight up. Still resting back on the lounge chair, her mother turned her head. "Just in case."

Slowly, Hayley nodded. She needed to check Finn's diaper, then put him to the bassinet next to her bed, and then finally sleep herself.

"Maybe I'll take some lessons, too," she said.

A new life, a new baby, a new name ... and a killer attitude.

6

Inside her oceanfront home, Polina pressed her hands on each side of her head. Rage and sorrow burned through her. Like an old cartoon, she was sure that steam must be gusting out of her ears, and if she didn't calm down, the top of her head would blow off.

She was alone in her twelve-thousand-square-foot home, so no one was around to hear her screaming and raging and swearing in Russian. So much more satisfying than English, but since she was still angry and hurt and sick inside her heart, she swore in English, too.

Still, it wasn't enough to cool the fiery wrath inside her. There was no one to see her as she threw a crystal vase at the wall, the vase shattering. No one to care that she ripped an oil painting of Leo off the wall, dropped it onto the tiled floor, then went to the kitchen to fetch a meat mallet, coming back to slam the mallet down on his picture and smash it and smash it and smash it. Not caring about the glass shards bouncing off her face.

Until finally, her arms sore, she dropped down onto her knees on the cold marble tiles, broken pieces of glass piercing her skin while she wailed and pounded her fists on the marble, only stopping when blood dripped off of her knuckles, her voice rasped, and her tears dried up.

But not her hate. Her hate intensified, simmering inside of her.

"I want to kill him," she whispered, her rasping voice as broken as her heart. "I want to pull out his heart, then speed to the Everglades and throw it into the mouths of alligators."

Even as she said the hateful words, her chest squeezed. She had loved Leo—maybe she still did, even though she now hated him. It was hard to turn the heart off like switching TV channels, but she knew now that the man she had thought was strong was, in reality, weak.

Not just weak but selfish and heartless.

Leo's mother had blamed her for the muck up. "You should have known he was a careless lover," Olga had said, sitting stiffly. "Just like his father."

Polina had wanted to tell Olga that it was also her fault for spoiling Leo. For allowing him to get away with so much. Damn Olga for not making him accountable for his actions. Damn her for not being sterner, the way that Polina's mother had raised her.

And damn Leo's father for being an arrogant womanizer. Leo's role model.

With an example like his father, how could Leo have been any different?

In the end, both parents had turned on her. Blamed her. Even Leo. Because she might be barren. As if not popping a baby out of her vagina the first seven years of her marriage marked her as damaged.

As if Leo hadn't been eager to fuck that woman who was a pale imitation of her.

She pounded the marble floor again, weak sounds coming out of her mouth, bitter tears tracking down her cheeks.

Until, finally, she wiped the tears away.

She needed to stop this. She needed a plan.

She pushed up, sitting on the floor of the huge, empty house where even her breath seemed to bounce back at her.

Her heated emotions cooled, allowing her to think coherently. This last year she'd done exactly what Leo had wanted to do. Because of him, she had no husband in her home now. No baby in her arms. People angry at her for Leo's stupid idea.

At least the Feds hadn't charged her with anything. In her earliest texts, she had begged him not to go ahead with the scheme. Only when she knew he was seeing the woman without her permission had she reluctantly agreed to go along with Leo's plan.

It had broken her heart, and now she realized she had been stupid. Stupid with love.

She vowed to never love again. Never allow a man to make plans for her without her full agreement. From now on, her decisions were going to be her own.

She had money, quite a bit, though if she remained in this place too long, the money would drain away. Her in-laws blamed her for Leo's incarceration. They certainly wouldn't pay her bills.

Her own father blamed her, too. To him, she was a failure because she hadn't been able to breed on demand. Her mother was on drugs half the time, lying in her bedroom in a half daze. An addict, though people just called her *sick*, as her doctor prescribed drugs that he said were good for her nerves. When in reality, it was good for his bank account.

Damn him. Damn all men.

And what if Leo was right? What if she never had a baby? She was twenty-seven already. Still beautiful—so her mirror told her—but she was no longer the dewy twenty-year-old who had caught Leo's attention.

An ache started inside her heart that pounded hard.

She could still have any man she wanted, but she didn't want one. What she wanted was a baby.

Leo's baby, though that would never happen now.

Or would it?

Her breath caught. Her heart pounded faster and harder. If she found the baby, everyone would love her again. Leo's father. His mother. And Leo would love her—though she didn't care about him anymore.

She hated Leo. Hated him. Hated him. Hated him.

She was thinking of her future. Maybe thinking like a crazy woman, her thoughts in a jumble.

Should she? Shouldn't she?

She closed her eyes and imagined herself holding the baby. A calm settled inside her, and her breaths slowed.

She would love the baby.

The baby would love her.

Was it possible? Could she do it?

The pounding of her heart calmed. She opened her eyes and put her hands on both sides of her face. She didn't know how she was going to do this, or if it was even possible. But when she set her mind to something, she could make it happen. She always did.

And this time there would be no man to tell her what to do. This time—if she went through with it—*she* would be in charge.

Wes, his dog, and his uncle stepped into the pub…

The thought made Wes grin. It was the beginning of a joke, but for him it was real life about five days out of seven since he'd moved into his uncle's house.

The sun was lowering outside, and Wes was feeling pleased with his day. He'd been in his uncle's workroom most of the afternoon, making two lamps out of headlights from an old truck. Before this, he'd tried making a few different things. Chairs. Coffee tables. Cupboards.

Each one had felt like dating. One was horrible, two were all right, but none had made his chest thump. Nothing had felt *right*.

Until now...

Before they'd left the workshop, his uncle had said, "I think you've found your calling."

Wes didn't know if making lighting fixtures with headlights from vintage trucks and cars was important enough to be labeled a *calling*, but he couldn't stop grinning.

This was a count-your-blessings day for him. Compared to many other guys—and women—in his situation, he had it good. He gave thanks for his uncle and some great doctors and nurses. He'd already adjusted to walking with a below-the-knee prosthetic leg, and every day he told himself that he was lucky he was alive.

Sometimes he still woke up sweating and shuddering from a bad dream. Sometimes the blackness dropped down on him like bombs. A loud noise could have the same effect.

The psychiatrist at the Veterans Administration had marked Wes as having a mild case of post-traumatic stress disorder, telling him if he didn't freak out or feel like killing or maiming people, he was functional.

Right now, Wes believed that psychiatrist. Right now, he did feel almost normal. Right now, he felt as if he might even be a little better than functional.

"Hey, guys." Lucy, the pub owner's unmarried and pregnant niece, stopped off at their table. "Beer again?"

They nodded, then ordered dinner. On Wednesday, ribs were the special, and they both ordered a full rack with coleslaw and a potato. Curled up on the wooden floor next to Wes's chair, Spock huffed. By now, Spock knew what *ribs* meant. When they returned home, Wes would take his leftover ribs—usually at least three—out of the doggy bag, then pull the meat off and give it to Spock.

Spock was always happy on rib day. But Spock was happy every day. Wes suspected that dogs knew how to enjoy their lives better than humans did.

As Lucy strode away, Donny, who worked for the county,

swiveled around in his stool at the bar. Donny had prematurely gray hair, and he lived with his mother down the block from Wes.

"You seen your new neighbors yet?" Donny asked, his blue eyes bright with excitement.

"The white ranch?" Wes shook his head. He hadn't seen anyone in the house since last September, when two couples rented it for the summer. His uncle said the owner lived in Florida and rented it out to tourists in summer.

"That's it," Donny said.

"We just left the workshop fifteen minutes ago. We were there all day. I didn't know anyone moved in." As Wes finished speaking, he realized he sounded like a longtime resident, his tone aggrieved because he hadn't known about his new neighbors.

When he'd first settled in, he'd expected to be sitting in the house most days, staring at the TV and brooding, but the opposite had happened. By now, he knew most of the residents by sight and a few hundred by name.

"Two women moved in," Donny said. "Both blonds. My mom says she can tell it's not their natural color, but who cares? They're both lookers. The younger one has a baby. The older one's closer to my age. She's a knockout."

"Watch out for the knockouts," Blake said. "They're high-maintenance."

"Like me." Lucy plopped down a beer in front of him and another one for Blake.

Everyone laughed but Wes and Blake. As Lucy's face turned red, Wes put his hand on her upper arm.

"A knockout *exactly* like you," he said.

She sniffed. "You're a good man." Raising her voice, she called out, "Not like the other jerks here."

The volume of voices rose as she stalked away and apologies were shouted out to her.

"I didn't mean anything."

"I was just kidding."

"Lucy, I think you're beautiful. You can come over to my house any time. I'll show you how beautiful I think you are."

She was laughing before she got to the back, the door swinging behind her.

"I wonder what the two women are doing here," Donny said.

"It's a tourist town." Blake shrugged. "I imagine they came here to see the beautiful scenery."

"Or to paint the scenery." Wes grimaced. "Half the people who come here are wannabe artists. Including me now."

"Not wannabe," Blake said. "You *are* an artist."

Wes shook his head. He didn't feel like an artist. He was proud of his light fixtures, but it felt more like play than work. A part of him still felt purposeless. If not for Blake, he'd most likely be holed up in a small apartment in Chicago, and he didn't know what he'd be doing there. Taking classes online or learning a new skill. Or just staying home and sleeping away the days, fighting off bouts of depression.

Instead he was here in this small town with his uncle, his lifesaver. He couldn't give up or give in. His uncle had put too much work into him. He needed to live up to Blake's expectations.

Someday he'd be okay. Someday he'd help someone else the way his uncle had helped him. The way—

Darkness slashed down in his mind, like a shade lowering, blocking out the sunlight. He froze, hearing shouting voices and dust and the angry sounds of sniper rifles.

His hand tightened around the water glass, and he stared into grayness.

Spock whimpered and got to his four feet, resting his head on Wes's left thigh. Wes put his shaking hand on Spock's silky fur, the move automatic. His lungs that had sucked air in and then stopped breathing for a long moment, exhaled and then inhaled. Again and again and again...

I'm going to be all right. I'm going to be all right. I'm going to be all right. The darkness lifted slowly. In his head, he heard the fierceness in his raspy voice as the others talked and laughed, their words sounding if they were coming from far away. *I'm going to be okay. I'm a lucky man. A lucky man. A lucky, lucky, lucky man.*

He kept repeating the words in his mind. A mantra. Not taking his hand from Spock's neck.

"*You okay?*" Uncle Blake asked, the words sounding like they came from out of a fog. "*You okay, Wes?*"

Wes nodded, not turning his head, still sitting there with his hand on Spock's neck until the last strands of darkness drifted away and the strained muscles in his neck and arms and back eased. Slowly, he took his hand off Spock's neck and sat back.

Spock licked the back of his left hand, then lay down.

"You okay?" his uncle asked again.

Wes nodded. His hands were almost steady now.

"You sure?"

Wes nodded again. "I'm alive. I've got my dog. I'm eating. I have a place to live. I'm one of the lucky ones."

"Life boils down to the simple things. But you're missing something."

"What's that?"

Blake's eyebrows whipped upward. "A woman."

"No way." Wes shook his head. "Ain't gonna happen. Not for a long time."

His uncle clapped him on his back.

"If I were you, I wouldn't bet on it. Life is funny."

Wes shrugged and looked at the menu, but the printing was a blur, and he wondered about his new neighbors. He'd gotten used to not having neighbors on each side of his uncle's house. He hoped they wouldn't be noisy. The best-case scenario would be if he never saw them.

7

By the time Wes and Spock reached home, the dusky sky was streaked with gold and pink. He walked into the kitchen, not bothering to turn on the lights, then refreshed Spock's water and gave him the meat from two of the leftover ribs. He'd put the third rib in the fridge. He'd give it to Spock tomorrow.

He thought about getting a beer for himself, but he'd already had two, and that was his daily limit. During the daytime, he was busy and working, usually in his uncle's workshop, but most nights after he left the pub, he was alone, either reading a book or watching TV. He didn't want to pick up any destructive habits.

Some nights, his thoughts took over, and they weren't pretty. He would say aloud, over and over again, "I'm alive. I'm walking. I'm creating. I have Spock. My uncle is here for me. I have a place to stay, and I've made a few friends. I'm a lucky man."

Until finally the empty, twisting, whining self-pity would slip away. At least for that night.

He could feel that sickness seeping up inside him now. It didn't usually happen twice a day. Twice a week was the norm. Sometimes once. Sometimes he even skipped a week.

Maybe it was doubling down today because he'd finally created something unique. Something he was proud of. Something that made him feel that he was getting better. In the workshop, Uncle Blake had even slapped him on his back, saying, "Damn, that's good."

He'd had his high, and now it was draining away, the darkness creeping in again. He knew the signs. What happened in the pub had been a precursor. Sometimes the darkness meant nothing. It would go away, like a quick rainstorm.

Other times it came long and hard and pounding.

That was okay. He was a warrior, and part of being a warrior was to kill the demons, whether they came in the form of the enemy or his own mind.

"I'm strong," he said aloud. "And I'm well. Not whole but whole enough. I can walk and I have friends and a future. Women ask me out. More than I—"

He shut up. That wasn't a good angle. He'd been here nine months, and he hadn't once felt desire for any woman. He'd had his choices, too. Local women who'd let him know they were happy to reward him for his great service to their great country. And, yeah, he'd been counting. Eight single women and two married women.

He'd turned them all down, stumbling through it the first time and, after that, making lame excuses. They probably all thought he couldn't get it up. If so, they were wrong. His body was willing, but he wasn't ready for a relationship, even on his good days. In a community this small, he couldn't hop in bed with a woman just for sex.

What would he say to her the next day at the pub or the grocery store? Or what if she stopped off at Blake's workshop? Would he have to tell her that she was good enough for one time, but now that they'd had sex, he didn't want her? Like a tissue he no longer needed.

He just wasn't that guy.

His thoughts were making him restless. Maybe he should get a beer after all. He needed one tonight. But the thought that he *needed* one instead of *wanted* one made him head out of the kitchen. A soak in the bathtub would be more relaxing than a beer.

The shades in his bedroom were up, fading rays of sunlight dancing through the window. He didn't bother turning on the light as he pulled his T-shirt over his head, then tossed it on the chair in the corner. Once his T-shirt was off, a light came on in the house next door, in the room across from his bedroom window. It must be his new neighbors. He headed over to the window, expecting to see a… Well, he wasn't sure what he expected to see. After all, he—

Holy naked calendar girl.

A woman. She stood in front of the window, her head turned away from him. Not beautiful, but pretty. A blond with straight hair that reached her shoulders. There was a reddish tint to her blond hair, but his gaze was already sliding downward. She was naked, at least from the hips up. And she was touching her breasts. Massaging them, as if they were sore.

He stepped closer to the window. If he were any closer, his nose would be pressed against it, like a kid staring at toys in a store window.

His body was reacting to the view. Now her hands left her plump breasts and moved downward to… Well, he couldn't see where her hands were heading, but his imagination was filling in the blanks.

Then she did something he didn't expect.

She turned her head. Looking straight at him.

He stopped breathing. Her room had the lights on, not his. Chances were that she couldn't see him. In fact, he'd bet money that she wouldn't see him.

She stood still for a long moment. He finally exhaled. Slowly. Trying not to make a motion that she might see. If she could see him through the window, maybe she would think he was a picture or a movie poster or—

Her lips pressed together. Her eyes narrowed. She held up her hand and gave him the finger, then reached up and pulled her blind down.

He slowly reached up and pulled down his shade. As he turned away, he started to laugh. And laugh some more. And then laugh so hard that he had to sit down on his bed. Laughing so hard his stomach hurt and he bent forward, his laughs coming out in short bursts now. Finally, he stopped, sitting up as he sucked in his breath and then exhaled again.

Then another noise came out of his throat, this one harsh and ugly. He tried to hold it back, but the noise wouldn't stop, and it wasn't laughter anymore. It was tears. The sound of sorrow. He put his hand over his eyes and bent forward and cried. And cried. And cried.

At the side of his bed, Spock whined. Finally, Spock crawled up on the bed, a place he'd been trained to stay away from. Instead of telling Spock to get down, Wes put his arms around Spock's strong neck, and he rocked back and forth for what seemed like a long, long time.

When he finally stopped, he felt emptied of … something. Self-pity maybe. Grief. Horror. All of that. As if he'd laughed and then cried an immense stash of emotion out of him.

He released Spock, who jumped down to the carpeted floor, then looked up at him. The sky had turned dark, Spock's black body blending into the grayness, but Wes could see the whites of Spock's eyes, his teeth shining in his open mouth, and even the pink of his tongue.

Another raw emotion built up inside Wes. Gratitude.

He was alive. He'd lost one limb, and it wasn't even a full limb, just half a limb.

How many other servicemen and women had much worse injuries? How many others were as lucky as him to be given a free place to stay? How many had a family member or a friend watching over them? Who was there for them? How many had a dog like Spock, whose sole purpose was to watch over him?

Not just servicemen and women. How many non-military men and women? How many—

He sucked in a breath and stopped his thoughts that were running on in a different sort of self-pity.

He was okay. He was one of the lucky ones.

Slowly, he stood and leaned over to rub the top of Spock's smooth head.

Someday, he would pay this back. Someday, he would help another person, whether they were in the service or just in a bad place.

Not tonight, though. Tonight his energy was drained out of him, and he'd be lucky to help himself.

"I'm tired," he said. "How about you?"

Spock tilted his head.

Wes nodded and straightened. "I thought so. You're a smart dog."

The nights were still cool, and he closed all the windows, then brushed his teeth. Forget the soak in the tub. He could shower tomorrow.

Lastly, he put Spock outside one more time. As he did all this, he thought of the woman next door. She probably wouldn't want to talk to him ever, but he wondered if she was married.

He called Spock back in, then crawled into his bed. The heavy curtain of sleep was coming down on him. As his thoughts darkened and emptied, an image of his neighbor's breasts flashed into his mind. Her beautiful rounded breasts.

Smiling, the bad stuff emptied from his mind, he toppled into slumber.

8

FINN'S CRYING WOKE HAYLEY OUT OF A DEEP SLEEP. THE room was dark, and she forced herself to wait, in case he might go back to sleep. According to the pamphlets and books she'd been reading, this was part of his development at three months.

But his cries didn't stop and instead grew louder. With a sigh, she rolled out of bed, turned on the light, and picked him up out of the new bassinet next to her bed.

Finn wanted his mama.

She changed his diaper quickly, already an expert at the art of diaper changing, then scooped him up, his damp face against her neck, his skin warm and soft, his little fingers opening and closing against her shoulder. His cries softened and slowed, turning into tiny sobs, then small hiccups of sounds.

"Sweet baby boy," she whispered. "My sweet boy."

Looking around, she wished there were a rocking chair in the house. He had been sleeping through the night the last few days, but this move and the different time zone might have disturbed his sleep pattern. Until he got used to the change, it wouldn't hurt to—

His cries stopped, his breaths even. He was sleeping. She waited a couple minutes before putting him back into the bassinet. He made a sound, and she put her hand on his neck, murmuring his name, giving him the connection that coursed between them. The sound stopped, and she waited a minute before slowly pulling her hand away.

"I love you," she whispered, bending over the bassinet. "Your grandma loves you. We're going to give you a wonderful life and watch you grow and play and learn and become a great man someday. Even better than great, you'll be a good man. A loving man. You'll always know that you are loved and cherished."

Then she turned and headed to the hallway, not surprised that her mom was waiting in the hall, smiling with tears welling up in her eyes.

"That's how I love you, too," Susan murmured, and she reached out to hug Hayley for a moment before pulling apart.

"Mom, you are the best. You uprooted your life for me—"

"Don't be silly." Her mother wrinkled her nose. "I did it for me. I always wanted to live in a small town."

"Bullshit. In fact"—Hayley put her hands on her hips over the soft cotton T-shirt gown that stopped above her knees—"you didn't even know we were coming to a small town."

"Just a little lie." Her mother held up her thumb and forefinger that almost touched.

"A little lie. A lot of laughter."

"Absolutely. And everything we did, it will be worth it."

They grinned at each other in the dimness of the hallway, with the nightlight from the bathroom gleaming into the hall. Her mother gave her one more quick hug, then released her and headed back to her room.

Hayley crossed to the bathroom, returning to her bed a few minutes later. Being a new mom was exhausting, and today she'd been on a long plane ride from Florida to Madison, Wisconsin, and then they'd had a three-and-a-half-hour drive to Trouble Bay. Her butt had been numb from all that sitting. Her mind felt numb, too.

She wasn't surprised. This last year, her life had changed drastically. Her former lover had used her to be a baby maker for his barren wife, then he'd planned to kill her so they could keep the baby for their own. Or, alternately, he would just steal the baby and tell her that it had died. No one knew that part for sure, but just thinking about it, she felt sick.

Leo would likely be in prison for at least a dozen years. His wife, Polina, obviously had known what he'd been up to, but her texts had showed enough reluctance for her to stay out of jail. Instead she was given a period of one year of unsupervised probation, which was like a slap on her hand.

Hayley sighed, then reminded herself that she had the prize. She had what Leo and Polina had ached for, had schemed for. She had Finn.

What happened to Leo's wife was not her problem. In one of Leo's texts to his wife, he'd said he'd searched for months for someone special to be their baby mama. Someone smart and pretty and funny, and most of all, someone with auburn hair, the same color as Polina's.

Yuck. Now her hair was blond with a strawberry tint. It was unlikely that anyone from the Russian Mafia would be in Trouble Bay, but if they were, she and her mother would be two blond women. No one would point their finger at them.

"We'll make it work," Hayley whispered, her head turned to the bassinet. "I won't let anyone take you from me. Not until you're a grown man and it's your decision."

Finn didn't reply, his breaths soft in sleep. Hayley closed her eyes. The truth was that she wasn't good with men. She was too practical, too boring—and sometimes too easily bored.

Leo hadn't exactly bored her, but near the end, she hadn't liked him enough to continue their relationship. At first, she'd been attracted to him. What woman wouldn't be? He was handsome and wealthy, and he definitely wanted her. But then she'd realized he was too … macho, perhaps. Or selfish. Yes, that was the word. Too much *me* and not enough *you.*

Her instincts had nailed him, but it was too bad she hadn't realized that a few weeks sooner.

She sighed. Maybe someday she would love a man who wasn't her father or her son, but right now she was pretty sure that wasn't going to happen for a long, long time.

Then she thought of the man next door and rolled her eyes. *Pervert.* Certainly it wouldn't be someone like him.

WES DREAMED OF HIS MOTHER. She was smiling at him, laugh lines crinkling the corners of her eyes. She didn't say anything, just looked at him. Waiting. He had something to tell her, something to *ask* her, but he couldn't think of what it was. Instead he just thought, *I love you. I miss you.*

She continued to smile. Though her mouth didn't open, he could feel the love in her eyes, as if she were sending him ten times more love than when she was alive.

Right back at you, he shouted into the silent night. *Right the heaven back at you.*

WAKING UP, Wes immediately remembered the dream—and the woman next door. He stared at the ceiling and wondered if they were somehow connected, though he knew it wasn't possible. His mother was dead. That part had been a dream. The woman in the next house hadn't been a dream. Her breasts had been very real.

Still lying in bed, he closed his eyes and pictured her breasts in his mind. So round and full and perfect. He wasn't a breast man, though that didn't mean he didn't like them. Of course he *liked* breasts. He appreciated them. The slight weight and the softness. The way nipples hardened against his palm. But they weren't the main event. They were just a warm-up for the important part farther down.

And from the woman's reaction, he was sure she would be more careful in the future, and he wouldn't see her breasts again. Too bad. He wanted to see them. Not in a sexual way, but in an aesthetic way. The same way he would view a piece of art. It didn't mean he wanted to purchase the art piece or touch it or do anything but look at it.

And the fact that his penis was springing up had nothing to do with her. That was still his morning thing. And thank God for that.

Spock was awake now, breathing hot air on the side of his face. Wes greeted Spock with a grunt, then sat up. He sniffed his underarms and decided they didn't smell enough for him to need a shower. Instead, he put on the clean briefs that he'd left at the chair next to his bed, and then his prosthetic leg, and then his jeans and a blue T-shirt. By the time he was done with all of that, his penis had settled down, realizing there was going to be no action this morning. Barefoot, he walked down the hall to the side door and let out Spock.

After using the bathroom, he went back to his bedroom to put a sock on his one foot. His prosthetic already had a sock on it. Since it never sweated, he didn't need to change it every day. Then he pulled up his window shade. Instead of turning away, he stood for a moment and gazed at the window across from him.

As he did, the blind pulled up in the other house. *Her* house. Before he had a chance to move, he was staring at the woman again. She wore some kind of a top that draped over her plump breasts in a perfect way. Or maybe it was just her breasts that were perfect. No bra. He wasn't an expert, but he knew enough to tell she was braless.

Once again, his body reacted.

She narrowed her eyes, looking straight at him, and she

mouthed something. Something short with two syllables. Like *pervert.*

Then she snapped around and tramped away.

His mouth watered. He would never look at plump fruit the same way again.

As she neared the doorway, she looked behind her.

Knowing she spotted him still staring at her, he groaned.

She swung around again, and as she stepped out of the room, she raised her arm up behind her head. Her middle finger stuck up.

He should feel guilty, but instead he laughed so hard he bent over and grabbed the windowsill to keep from toppling onto the bedroom rug. Finally his laughter died, and he could stand without support again.

Grinning, he left the bedroom to let Spock in. Sometime today, he'd have to go over to see the woman and let her know that he wasn't a pervert or a sex maniac. Maybe when he met her in person, he'd hate her voice or she'd say something silly or angry or she'd smell bad. Maybe something about her would put him off.

Or maybe she would notice that he'd lost part of his leg, though he only had a slight limp that people told him was hardly noticeable. She might hear about it from one of the townsfolk. She might be repelled, though none of the the women in Trouble Bay seemed to care. Of course, that could be because single or unattached men his age were sparse around here.

But this neighbor might be different. After all, she'd recently had a baby, and as far as he could see—as far as the locals knew—it was just her and another woman. There was no man around. Not that there was anything wrong with that, but she might not have a high opinion of men. She definitely didn't have a high opinion of him. Not after she'd caught him peering through the window at her. Not just once but twice.

Maybe she would look down her nose at him and tell him to eff off, holding up her middle finger again. Nothing to do with his leg. Just something to do with him being a pervert.

He opened the door for Spock, grinning at his thoughts that were nothing at all like his usual morning decision to do his best to get through the day without anger or pain or depression.

No, this time he didn't feel any of that. He felt different. As if anything could happen. Probably nothing would, but now there was an anticipation, a buzzing under his skin. Before this there had been one path for him. Now there seemed to be a few. And he wondered which path he would take...

9

"We have a Peeping Tom." Hayley sat on a chair at the kitchen table, holding Finn against the towel draped over her shoulder, rubbing his back. He burped out a sour-smelling rush of warm liquid onto the towel. After a few seconds, she changed his position, holding him so he was looking up at her. "You'll never be a Peeping Tom, will you? Huh, sweetie, will you?"

He waved his fist in the air and gurgled.

"He's saying he probably will," her mother said, putting aside the book she'd been reading. "If there's something to peep at, most men will not look away."

"Unless they're gay."

"*Please*." Susan rolled her eyes. "For some reason I can't fathom, gay men love to look at women's breasts. At least the ones I've known." She leaned over the table. "So, who's the peeper? A neighbor?"

"The house next door." Hayley gestured toward the peeper's house.

"What does he look like?"

"Um. Well, good. But that doesn't make it any less creepy."

Her mother laughed. "What does *good* mean? What does he look like? How old is he?"

"I'd guess early thirties. Brown hair. I couldn't make out his eye color. Straight nose and strong jaw, though not *too* strong. Kind of like an action hero face. The strong, silent type."

"You noticed a lot about him through the window."

"Since I was almost naked, he noticed a lot more about me."

"No!" Her mom laughed.

Hayley nodded, her lips pressed together, her nose wrinkling. "Oh, yes. I should have been more careful, but I didn't expect anyone to be there. When I saw him staring at me, I was too surprised to back away. *He* didn't back away, either."

Susan laughed with delight.

"You'll probably see him soon enough," Hayley said. "When you do, you can tell me what you think."

"I'll definitely tell you what I think." Susan stood, her chair legs scraping the floor. "In the meantime, how do you want your eggs?"

"You don't have to make breakfast for me."

"I don't have to, but I need to do *something*."

Hayley made a downward-dog face, feeling guilty. If she hadn't been so gullible, her mother would still be in Miami, having fun with her friends and making money in an occupation she was very good at. In this tiny town, Hayley doubted she or her mother would make anywhere near what they had earned in Miami. Or if they could even find a job. The witness protection service wasn't going to support them forever.

She didn't say any of this to her mother. If she did, her mother would tell her once again that she'd *wanted* to come here with her. She'd insisted. And none of what happened had been Hayley's fault. She was the innocent party.

Maybe that was all true—or mostly true. But a little bit was her fault for believing Leo.

For being stupid.

"*Stop.*" Susan frowned at her. "Stop right now. I can see you mentally berating yourself, and don't be silly. We are going to *love* this place. It's beautiful here. I love the green grass and the trees. And I'm actually looking forward to snow. And the prices! Everything costs so much less here."

"Honestly, Mom?"

Her mother put her hand over her left breast. "Honest."

Hayley nodded. Her mother was a brilliant liar. So good that she almost believed her.

"So, do you want scrambled eggs or over easy?" Susan asked.

"Scrambled is fine." She strapped Finn into his bouncy chair and set it on the table. Since the table wasn't real wood, she doubted the bouncer would scratch it.

"I'll have the same." Susan bent over Finn and changed her voice, softer and singsongy. "Yes, Grandma will have an egg and fruit for breakfast, just like Mama. Doesn't that sound like fun?"

He gurgled and his hands and legs jiggled. Susan kissed him on the forehead, and he gurgled again.

"Finnegan is the sweetest baby ever." Susan straightened, looking at Hayley. "Except you when you were three months old."

"You're not prejudiced at all, are you?" Hayley laughed. "I'm lucky to have *you* as a mom. Finn is lucky, too."

Her mother crossed to the refrigerator and opened the door, bending to take out eggs. "Tell me more about the Peeping Tom."

"That's about it. From now on, I'll pull the blind down. I'm taking the blame for that. But once he saw that I saw him, he should have stepped away."

"Actually, sweetie"— her mom set the eggs on the counter—"he probably couldn't do it. Not swiftly anyway."

"Because it would hurt his hard-on?"

Her mother laughed and didn't stop until she had to grab a paper napkin to wipe tears from her cheeks.

Finn laughed with her, and Hayley chuckled, too.

"His hard-on wasn't quite what I had in mind, though I'm sure that was part of his problem," Susan said. "Someone at the grocery store told me that our new neighbor was in the army, and he lost his left leg beneath his knee."

Hayley's laughter stopped, and she stared at her mother.

"His uncle had bought a cabin by the lake as an investment," Susan continued. "He was planning to rent the cabin during the tourist season. Instead, he moved into it and told his nephew he could live in the house."

"Wow. Now I almost feel guilty for giving him the finger."

Her mom chuckled, then turned to the stove.

"Maybe," Hayley said, "I can make it up by flashing my breasts at him again."

They both cracked up. "Great idea," her mom finally said, gasping.

That stopped Hayley's laughter. "You're kidding, right?"

"I should be. You're my daughter." Susan shrugged. "I've always been conflicted about upper body nudity for women and not men. After all, covering women's breasts is a cultural thing. When the weather permits, men don't hide their often hairy chests—which is often accompanied by a sagging beer belly. Now, *that* should definitely be covered."

"I agree." Hayley nodded. "There should be a law against that."

"With huge fines."

"And right now," Hayley said, "my breasts are being used for the most necessary of all reasons—breakfast, lunch, dinner, and snack time. Yet I'm supposed to cover mine. It makes no sense."

"The laws are made to protect us from the lust of men." Her mother rolled her eyes. "Funny that it's men who make most of those laws. I think the whole thing about women's upper nudity is because men don't want to see our breasts when they start sagging."

"Thank you for that lovely thought. Let's change the subject, please."

"Okay. I'm going to look for a job today." Susan cracked an egg into a bowl, then another one.

Hayley stared at her mother. As usual, her mom was going too fast for her. "What kind of a job?"

"I thought I'd talk to someone in real estate—"

"We aren't supposed to sign up for the same jobs we did before." As soon as the words flew out of her mouth, Hayley cringed. Her mother had enjoyed being a Realtor ... except for the hours and working weekends. And sometimes the people were unpleasant. But no job was perfect, and Hayley knew that if it weren't for her bad taste in men, her mother would be in Miami, breaking sales records for another year.

"I know you're feeling guilty," Susan said. "Stop it! I've thought of something I'll enjoy more than selling real estate to unpleasant people."

Hayley stared at her mother.

"Staging houses," Susan said. "I've wanted to try it but didn't have time. To be honest, I wasn't sure how well I'd do. I'm not trained in design, but in my real estate career, I've seen homes transformed by a few simple changes. I'd like to give it a shot. What do you think?"

Hayley saw her mother's vulnerability. Her uncertainty. "You have the *best* taste of anyone I know. You should do it. You'll be a fabulous stager."

Her mother laughed, the sound a shade too high and too nervous. "It takes a bit of magic to successfully stage a house, and I don't know if I have that magic touch. Before I start, I need to check out resale shops to see what they have. A nice couch or settee. A few chairs, tables, lamps, and pictures. A mix of styles. As soon as I have that, I might talk to different Realtors and see what they say."

"That's a wonderful idea! And if you decide that staging houses isn't right for you, we can use some of what you find for ourselves." Hayley swept her arm out to encompass the ranch house, then added quickly, "Not the ugly brown recliners, of course. They're too comfortable to give away."

Susan shook her head. "No, we wouldn't give them away—well, not give them away, since this isn't our house, but put them in the basement. Instead of doing that, I'd like to paint them."

"Really? Painting chairs?"

"Really. Google it! A neighbor's daughter in my condo painted two chairs for her mother. She used fabric paint. Ever since I saw her chairs, I wanted to try it."

"What if Finn spits up on the couch, like sour milk?" Hayley pointed at Susan. "Or you with your chocolate? Or red wine? Or if it's a hot day and melted food dribbles onto the couch, and we wipe it off, will the paint wipe off, too?"

Susan laughed. "That shouldn't happen. You worry too much. If it doesn't work, I'll pay the landlord for new chairs."

"If it happens, I'll pay for the chairs," Hayley said, reminding herself that her mother could be in Miami with the bright lights and the shows and shops and her many friends. Instead she was here in this small town that was too quiet and too cold. The least Hayley could do was to support her mother in anything that might make her happy. "This sounds intriguing."

"I think so, too. We can even make our own fabric paint. I'm sure I can find directions online. Or a YouTube video! It will be much cheaper than paying someone to do it."

"If that's what you want to do, I think we should give it a shot."

Her mother's face lit up, and she looked so vibrant that Hayley had to blink back tears. "This is going to be a good thing for us," Hayley said, hearing the thickness of her voice.

"As long as we have each other and our health," her mother said, "we can *make* it into a good thing."

Hayley nodded. She'd been impregnated without her permission, she'd had to testify in court, change her identity, move across the country—and what hurt the most was that she didn't know if she'd ever see her father again.

But her mother was with her, and she had Finn, who she loved more than she'd ever thought she could love another being.

"And you know what's the *best* part of this?" Hayley asked.

"What?"

"We get to go shopping!"

Her mother laughed, and so did Hayley, though she didn't have her mother's sense that something good was going to happen. Her mother might say that Hayley should think positive, but if she'd thought positive when she'd been dating Leo, she wouldn't have stood in the hallway and listened to him on the phone. She wouldn't have waited for him to leave. She wouldn't have read his texts and taken pictures of them.

Most of all, she very likely wouldn't be alive and holding her baby in her arms.

Negative thinking and a suspicious mind had saved her life.

"Why are you smiling?" her mother said. "Are you thinking of Mr. Peepers?"

Hayley laughed and slapped her thighs. The baby gurgled.

Chuckling, Susan went to the stove and turned on a burner. As she did, Hayley's laughter slowed until she wasn't laughing anymore. Because it seemed to her that with every positive came a negative. A yin and a yang. Lightness and darkness. Love and hate.

She hoped she was wrong, but she didn't want to be dead wrong.

10

"HE CAN'T SEE YOU NOW." POLINA'S FATHER-IN-LAW'S assistant was rigid with impatience.

Polina's heart was broken, her spirit cracked, and this prune-faced woman was giving her the evil eye because she wasn't shriveling up and slinking away.

She hadn't wanted to come here, but she'd had no choice.

She stood. The hell with her father-in-law. If he wouldn't listen to her, it was his loss.

Her lips set tightly, Polina whirled and strode down the hallway of her father-in-law's luxury offices, the four-inch heels of her shoes tapping on the tiled floor.

She was wasting her time here. She understood what was happening. She was the scapegoat. And everyone knew what happened to the scapegoat.

As she hurried down the hallway, two big, burly men hugged the wall, as if fearful of getting too close to her. Perhaps afraid that someone would snap a picture of her and they would accidentally be in the picture.

After that, they would accidentally be killed. Because people in the Russian mob knew that accidents happened all the time. Accidents that led to death.

Right now they thought that Polina was an accidental death about to happen.

Polina ignored them, her head high. She believed in the adage that if one road was blocked, then find another road.

She knew the one man who would nudge her down that road like no one else could. The one man whom Peter, her father-in-law, had admired yet distrusted. A man who Peter had once said was too smart. Peter didn't trust smart people.

Polina didn't trust anyone right now, but she was desperate, and he might be her last chance.

BREAKFAST WAS OVER, and Hayley's mother was sitting on the tan couch, looking at paint colors on her cell phone. "You know what color I'd like?"

"Green." Lying on the floor, facing Finn, who lay stomach-down on his soft baby blanket, Hayley raised her voice two octaves higher than normal. "You like green, don't you, sweetie?"

Finn slapped his hand on the blanket and babbled something that could have been *green*. Or any word.

"Are you a baby?" Hayley asked. "The cutest baby in the whole world?"

Finn slapped his hand on the blanket again and gurgled a laugh.

"I love you. You're a sweetheart." She slid the tip of her middle finger down his little nose and earned another happy gurgle.

"Green goes so well with our hair." Susan lifted her hand and fluffed up her blond hair. "Even though we're mostly blond now. And look at the grass growing outside. Who doesn't like green grass?"

"The grass looks more yellow than green to me."

"Not all of it. In a week or two, it will be all green." Her mother's eyelids lowered, her chin raised, and her nostrils flared, as if smelling the freshness of new grass. "A beautiful grass-green color. And the trees will all have leaves. Already, I've seen a lot of buds on trees."

"You want to paint the couch and the recliners grass green?" Hayley asked.

Finn wailed and slapped his hand on the carpet, clearly wanting her attention again.

"I think I'll leave the couch alone for now and just do the recliners. I'm thinking of a pretty light green," Susan said. "It's a happy color. The color of a new beginning. Perfect for you and me and Finnegan."

Hayley pushed up, crossed her legs, then leaned over and picked up Finn, who waved his hand in the air, happy noises bubbling from his throat. "You've always had good taste. If you say it will look good, I'll believe you. But will our landlady like it?"

"There's only one way to find out." Susan picked up her cell phone.

A minute later, Hayley was blowing bubbles on Finn's neck, and he was waving his hand in the air, sometimes connecting with her head, and making happy noises as Susan talked to their landlady, the enthusiasm in her voice hard to resist.

"Thank you!" she said at last, her eyes bright. "I promise, if you dislike the color, I'll redo the recliners in brown again."

Hayley groaned.

Susan and their landlady talked for another few minutes, then her mother clicked off. "Done!"

Hayley nodded and smiled. That was the big difference between her and her mother. Her mother believed that everything would turn out better than before. Hayley just hoped that it wouldn't end up as a total disaster.

Like her relationship with Leo. He hadn't broken her heart. She'd been angry and scared and even sickened, but she'd never been heartbroken. An old boyfriend had accused her of waiting for something better, but that wasn't true, either. The truth was that she wasn't sure if there *was* anything better.

But now, as she looked down at Finn, cradling him in her arms with so much love inside her, she knew *he* was her something wonderful. *He* was the love of her life.

Who needed a man? Not her.

"You want to come to the paint store with me?" Susan asked.

Hayley wrinkled her nose. "As exciting as that sounds, I think I'll pass."

Her mother laughed, then headed to her room to change her top that had a sour-milk dribble on it, thanks to Finn. Hayley followed behind her, turning into her bedroom to change Finn's diaper, calling out, "I'm going to take Finn for a walk."

"Maybe you'll meet our neighbor in person," Susan called.

"That will be so lovely. I'm sure a Peeping Tom is a step up from the last guy. The one who wanted to kill me."

Susan's laughter trilled out. Her mom always did have a macabre sense of humor that Hayley must have inherited, because she was grinning. She'd had her season of anger and coldness. Now she was starting her own season of healing and warmth.

"At least our life isn't boring," she said to Finn as she changed his diaper.

She added a gray long-sleeved top to wear with her black slacks. Boring but slimming, and she still wanted to lose seven pounds of pregnancy weight. During their walk, maybe she'd meet a few neighbors who weren't perverts.

Only a couple feet from the house, Finn fell asleep in the reclining stroller. She raised her head and sniffed. The air was fresh with a cool edge, though the sun shone brightly. The tree in their front yard didn't have all its leaves on display yet, and the grass was more yellow than green. But she spotted signs of new life poking up from the ground. A lot like her mother's life, her life, and Finn's life.

A door clicked shut on the house next door. Her neck and

shoulders stiffened, and she heard the clip of dog feet stepping in time with the scuff of her neighbor's shoes. Reaching the main sidewalk, she steered the stroller in the opposite direction of her neighbor's house.

"Hey!" a man's voice called.

Him. Of course it was him. In three seconds, she ran two scenarios through her mind. One: she kept walking away, refusing to confront him. Two: she would turn around and hear what he had to say.

She slowed and stopped and finally turned around. Her first impression of her neighbor was *nice*. Her Peeping Tom neighbor had short, light brown hair, a square jaw, and a blade of a nose. Very manly. Unlike Leo, who'd worn the latest of men's styles, there was nothing distinguished about his clothes—a gray flannel shirt, black jeans, and brown hiking boots. She guessed he was four or five inches taller than her five-foot-six height.

She forced herself not to stare at his legs, though she recalled that he had a prosthetic leg, and she was pretty sure it was the left one. The dog, though, was safe to look at. A black lab, its mouth open in a happy smile.

Her neighbor stopped in front of her and looked a few inches down at her with his dark brown eyes that were almost the same color as his dog's eyes. "I'm sorry," he said, as his dog stopped next to him.

She lifted her chin. "What exactly are you apologizing for?"

"For, um, staring at you."

"You're sorry you did it?"

Two deep lines indented between his eyebrows. "I'm sorry I made you feel uncomfortable."

"So, you're *not* sorry you did it? That's not much of an apology."

"It didn't happen on purpose. Once I saw you, I should have stepped away."

"But you didn't." She sighed. He was manning up. She could

see he was embarrassed and ill at ease but apologizing anyway. She should give him a break, but she was still feeling hostile after her experiences in court, with Leo's lawyers trying to make what had happened *her* fault.

"And this morning, you peeked at me again," she added.

"I wouldn't call it peeking."

She raised her eyebrows.

"I looked out my window," he said, "opening the shades like I do every morning, and there you were." He winced. "That's a lousy excuse. I should have turned away. I apologize for that, too."

She stared at him, not knowing what to say. Then a loud cry came from behind her. Finn. He'd woken up, and he wanted his mommy.

She twisted around and picked him up, murmuring nonsense words as she held him against her shoulder. In the middle of a cry, he suddenly stopped, his eyes closed, a tear glimmering on his cheek. Rocking him, she softly sang the first two verses of "Hush, Little Baby." Humming, she settled him back in the stroller, then turned to face her neighbor.

"Don't do it again. I don't want to keep the blinds closed during the day. I like the sunlight, but I'll try to remember to keep my clothes on when the blinds are open. Just so you know, the reason women have breasts is *not* to excite men. It's not a sexual thing." She sighed, because she didn't want to have this conversation. And this man … he seemed genuine, but she couldn't forget that she had trusted Leo—and look what had happened there. "The real function of breasts is so women can feed babies. And I happen to have a baby."

"I agree. You shouldn't have to hide your breasts, especially in your own house. Especially when you're feeding your baby." He nodded, his expression serious. "Which is, as you said, the reason for breasts. So you don't really have to pull the blinds down on my account."

She stared at him, and he grinned.

He looked cute when he grinned.

She laughed finally, and even as she shook her head, she said, "In that case, maybe I won't pull them down. Good-bye, Mr. Peepers."

A rusty laugh cracked out of his throat, giving her the impression that he didn't laugh often. "It's Harding. Wes Harding. You can call me Wes."

"And your dog?" She glanced down at the Labrador retriever at Wes's side. "Does your dog have a name?"

"Spock. He's the best." He bent slightly and rubbed a floppy dog ear. "What about you and the baby? Do you have names?"

"I'm Hayley, uh, Perry, and my baby is Finn, short for Finnegan."

"Is there a Mr. Perry?"

"I'm sure there must be a Mr. Perry somewhere, but I haven't met him."

He released the dog's ear and straightened, his attention on her. "If you need anything, just call me."

"Something a *man* would do?" She felt a rush of heat. "I mean, with tools or ... well, something like that?" She closed her eyes and held back a groan.

"I have tools," he said softly.

Her eyes opened. "I think my brains are leaking out along with my breast milk, but I still have enough brain matter left to *not* ask what you mean by that. You have a good day."

As she strode away, she heard him chuckle. She should have been embarrassed or angry, but instead she was holding back her own chuckles.

She felt like a teenager again. No, not a teenager. *A woman*. She wasn't sure if that was good or bad, but for the first time in a year, she felt like lifting her face up to the sky and laughing until her stomach hurt.

11

HARDWARE STORES WEREN'T SUSAN'S NORMAL territory. Neither were small towns, but that didn't slow her down. There seemed to be only two salesmen in the Sturgeon Bay hardware store, a short drive from Trouble Bay, and both salesmen were talking to other customers.

In another aisle, she saw a tall, lean man in blue jeans, his thick dark hair streaked with gray. He was reaching up to pull down a box of nails and seemed to know what he was doing and where things were.

She waited until the box was in his hands before speaking to him. "Excuse me."

He turned. His eyes were green and his chin looked almost as stubborn as the one she saw in the mirror every day. By the lines around his mouth and on his forehead, she guessed his age to be in his mid to upper fifties.

His thick eyebrows rose, and she realized she'd been assessing him too long, as if he were a dress she wanted to try on.

She smiled slowly. "Sorry, I was staring. I don't usually do that.

You should be on a magazine cover. A woodsman or a hunting catalog."

The skin around the corners of his eyes crinkled. "A manly magazine. I like that."

She laughed. Who knew she would find someone so delicious to flirt with here? She glanced down at his left hand. No ring.

"In case you're wondering, I'm single," he said, a sandpaper edge to his deep voice. "My name is Blake Schubert. And you?"

"Susan Perry. Never married."

"Not because you've never been asked," he said. Not a question but a statement.

"Perhaps." She shrugged. "I have a daughter and a grandson. We recently moved to Trouble Bay."

"Ah. You must be my nephew's new neighbors. Behind the bed and breakfast?"

"The big white house? Yes. I didn't know it was a B and B."

"Not anymore. It closed down after last Christmas. The townspeople still call it a B and B, but the owners have other plans for it." He leaned toward her. "What brought you to Trouble Bay? I heard you might be staying awhile. You don't look like a normal tourist."

"People are talking about us?"

He chuckled. "You sound surprised. You obviously haven't lived in a small town before. We don't need talk radio here. We have more than our share of nosy neighbors."

"Then it's good that we met. You can tell your neighbors that I'm a woman of mystery." Peering up a few inches, she guessed he must be about six feet tall. "I was looking for someone who works here, but I see that you're not wearing the apron with the big pockets."

"I know my way around the place. What are you looking for?" He waited a beat. "Whatever it is, I'll get it for you."

"Whatever it is? You think a lot of yourself, don't you?"

Now it was his turn to stare down at her, amusement in his

eyes. "Everyone should speak well about themselves. If we don't, who will?"

She laughed softly. "True."

"So you'll let me help you?"

"I would appreciate that very much." She smiled widely. She'd missed flirting with men. The marshals had been too stuffy to flirt, and she'd been worried about her daughter. Not really in a flirting mood. "I'm going to paint the upholstery on two recliners. I'm making my own chalk paint, and I'll need flat latex paint and calcium carbonate."

"Follow me."

KNOWING the woman was following him, Blake put a little swagger in his step, and he couldn't remember when he'd last felt the need to swagger. At least a few years. He liked it that she wasn't a young woman. Younger than him, he guessed, but not too much younger. She had the kind of beauty that would shine when she was in her nineties. She made him walk taller and feel younger.

It took them under ten minutes to gather her painting supplies, and he was sorry it was done so swiftly.

"Where are you from?" he asked.

"Um, Chicago." She smiled up at him, but he caught the twinge in her face, the short wrinkling of her nose. And then there had been the *um* before *Chicago*.

"I know Chicago," he said. "What part are you from?"

"Um, near the lakefront."

"Really? You must be one of the lucky ones. The lakefront is premium."

Her smile was strained. "My situation has changed since then. I prefer not to talk about it."

"Sure, I understand." He nodded, keeping his expression serious. She could have had a bad divorce, though she'd said she had never married.

Or she could be lying.

He knew Chicago accents. They were similar to Wisconsin accents, and hers wasn't Chicago or Wisconsin. It's possible that she'd moved to Chicago from another state, but usually people mentioned if they came from another state. She hadn't done that.

And then there were the two giveaways. The *ums*. If she was lying, she wasn't comfortable at it, which was good to know.

Not like him. *He* was a very comfortable liar.

"You seem like a city girl," he said, and that was true.

"*Girl?*" She laughed up at him with her eyes and her mouth, not seeming to care about laugh lines, though she was beautiful with them or without.

"You're staring," she said.

"You're right." He let the two words drawl out. "You're a mystery, and I've always loved a mystery."

She smiled slowly. "I'm not part of any mystery. Just a woman who wants to save money by painting two ugly recliners that look as if they're covered with mud." Her eyebrows quirked up. "And you're a man who's asking me a lot of questions."

"I'm a curious man, I admit it. I know that curiosity killed the cat, but I'm no cat."

"You're more of a dog, right?"

He chuckled. "An old dog, maybe. Would you like to have coffee with me before you start your project?"

She looked at his face for a long moment. He remained still, a slight smile on his face. Then she nodded and turned, pushing the cart ahead of her.

He wasn't finished with his shopping, but he followed her with his cart. He'd return later and pick up the rest of the supplies he needed.

He had his priorities, and right now it was a woman.

12

It was midafternoon when Yuri Petrov walked into the bar. Though Polina knew better, her heart beat a little fast as he strode toward her, as if he'd known she would be sitting at a table in the back of the dark bar.

She watched him closely, unsure whether this was a good move or the worst move. Despite his Russian name, Yuri was light-haired and blue-eyed. His mother wasn't Russian, just his dad. Not the kind of father who knew best. Polina had only seen Yuri once, about five years ago at the birthday party of his babushka. When Polina had asked Leo about him, he'd scowled and said Yuri was an independent.

Even now, she wasn't sure what that meant, but of all of the men in her husband's extended family, Yuri was the only one Leo had spoken about with a hard note in his voice.

And perhaps the only one who wouldn't be afraid to help her.

He'd filled out since his babushka's birthday. So had she, though she'd lost twelve pounds since the trial. As he reached the table, her nerves tightened, and she wondered if this was another huge mistake.

"You're thinking too much," Yuri said. "I can hear the thoughts screaming inside your mind. It's like the roar of an angry crowd."

"You can read minds?" She raised her eyebrows.

"You have too much emotion." His tone was dispassionate. "You look hungry and stressed. You should eat."

She stared into his blue eyes. He didn't look away, and she had the unsettling sense that he truly cared about her.

Of course, that wasn't true. He cared nothing for her, just as she cared nothing for him. If she'd been smart, she would never have called him. Never have set up this appointment. In fact, she could still stand up. Still leave.

But he was right that she was hungry. She hadn't eaten since breakfast—a half of a grapefruit and a small dish of Greek yogurt. And he was right that she was stressed. She'd been stressed for a year. Maybe she'd been stressed since she married Leo.

She picked up two menus from behind the napkin holder and handed one to him. She'd barely looked at hers when the waitress came. She ordered an iced tea and a cheese sandwich with avocado, just because she was looking at the cheese sandwich when the waitress arrived. He ordered a pulled pork sub and coffee.

"Why did you call me?" he asked. "What do you want?"

"Peace. Love. Prosperity. A puppy."

He chuckled, and the tightness inside her belly eased.

"A kitten?" he asked.

"Of course. A bunny rabbit would be nice, too."

He leaned over the table toward her. "And a baby?"

Her breath sucked in. She froze, and her teeth started to chatter. She grabbed her purse and started to get up. He reached out and clasped her wrist.

"I apologize. Sit down." He paused, but she remained half-standing and half-sitting. "Please."

Sucking in her breath, she nodded and sat back down. Over his head, she spotted the waitress heading toward their table. She straightened, and so did he, catching her cue. A second later, the waitress dropped off her tea and his coffee, plus two waters.

As they sipped, he talked about a blues concert he'd gone to. One of the singers was a favorite of hers. They talked about it, then other singers. He liked jazz, too. He said his mother had been a jazz lover.

Somehow that made him seem more human. More real. Though she relaxed, she wasn't ready to talk about her parents, who had disappeared during the trial. Probably afraid her in-laws would kick her out and leave her penniless. And more afraid that Peter would demand back the substantial amount of money he'd given them before the marriage.

The waitress left their table, and Yuri leaned toward her. "You're still not ready to talk. We'll wait until after we eat. You haven't been eating well, have you?"

"I've been eating just fine."

She could tell by the rueful twist of his lips that he didn't believe her. Too damn bad. As if he read her mind, he leaned back and talked about an art festival he'd been to. She nodded and listened, and even said she liked paintings of islands.

"You've done your homework," she added.

He stilled.

"You mentioned the music that I love. Then art, which I also love."

"Really?" He sat back, his eyebrows up. "How odd that we have the same tastes."

"You are so full of it."

"You've been talking to my sister, haven't you?"

She laughed and shook her head, feeling lighter. Happier. Almost flirty.

"I have an idea," he said. "You tell me what you want to talk about."

"Islands. It's possible that I sometimes fantasize about living on one." She shrugged. "Or I might be lying to you."

"You're not lying." His eyes narrowed, and he stared into hers, as if he were trying to look inside her mind. "Tell me about your favorite island. What does it look like? What's it like to live there?"

She didn't speak for a moment. All she could think of was that he was the first man who really *listened* to her. The first man who *heard* her. She had the feeling that he even read between the lines.

She talked about an island where she'd vacationed with her parents when she was so young that she couldn't remember the name. He kept asking questions, and she sat back as her imagination conjured up faint memories that she suspected probably had come from movies.

That didn't stop her from spewing out descriptions. The animals. The fish. The warmth. The friends. The dancing. The music. The food.

By the time the waitress returned with their sandwiches, her tension had left. It was all because of him. This man sitting across from her. As if he were playing her. She stared at him.

"What?" he asked.

She shrugged. She could get angry, but she couldn't gather enough anger to care. Maybe she liked being played.

They ate without speaking as Cuban music played from the bar's speakers.

"Why aren't you married?" She lowered her half-eaten sandwich.

He choked, and it gave her a sense of control.

"I once met a woman I wanted to marry." He looked straight at her. "But she was married to someone else."

"You are a huge flirt."

"Am I? Or am I telling the truth?"

"Seriously? I'm not here to flirt. I'm here because I have a job for you."

He sighed. "I was afraid of that."

She laughed, but it sounded brittle, and she stopped laughing and picked up her sandwich, then noticed that her hands shook.

She didn't know why, but it didn't matter. It wasn't important. Nothing mattered except the baby.

The baby was becoming an obsession. She couldn't seem to help herself. Thoughts of the baby filled her mind while her empty heart ached.

Yuri finished his pulled pork sub, then he sat back and watched her.

She set down the rest of her sandwich and raised her chin. "Are you ready to talk now?"

"I'm ready to listen," he said.

"Good answer. I need to find someone."

"And that would be..." His eyebrows rose in a question.

"The woman who testified against my husband. I need to find her. I need to find the baby."

"They're under the witness protection program. No one in the program has ever been found. Not unless they outed themselves."

"Things change. Everything is on computers now. We could find someone to hack into their database."

"No way in hell am I going down that route." His eyebrows came together. "The Feds could trace a hacker. I advise you against trying it. I won't do it."

She stared at him for a long moment. She wanted to scream, but of course she wasn't going to do that in this half-empty bar. Only a crazy person would do it. And she wasn't crazy. Not yet.

"There has to be another way," she said. "Can you do this, or am I wasting my time?"

"You're tougher than you look." He nodded, as if that pleased him. "The witness protection program is the US Marshals' baby. They're damn proud of it. They do a great job. Finding the mom and her son won't be easy."

"I've been told that you're a smart man. You figure it out."

He stared at her, not replying.

"I'll pay you. Name a price." She leaned forward. "You're a handsome man. You have ... I don't know. Sex appeal. Why not use that? Find a woman who works at the US Marshals Service. Pretend you're interested in her. She'll loosen up and talk about her co-workers. The people who work there are just like everyone else. They gossip. Find someone needy. Someone in trouble. Someone who's desperate."

"Like you're needy?" he asked. "Like you're desperate?"

"Damn you," she whispered, her hands balling into fists. "What do you want from me?"

He stared at her for a long moment. "What if I say that I want nothing from you? What if I said that I want you to be happy?"

She felt hot and then cold. "If you want me to be happy, then find the baby."

"If I agree, will *you* do what I say?"

She stared at him for what felt like a long moment, then she nodded. "Once I have the baby, I'll do whatever you want."

He put a fifty-dollar bill on the booth table. Standing, he looked down at her. "I'll hold you to that," he said, then he walked away.

Her breath stuck in her throat. She watched him stride past the bar to the door and open it. Gone. Only then did her breath puff out. She picked up his drink. The glass was a quarter full. She gulped it down. It wasn't beer but whiskey, the taste sharp, making her hiss. Then she took another gulp before setting the glass on the table.

She shimmied out of the booth and hurried outside. "The devil," she whispered to herself. She'd made a pact with the devil, and his name was Yuri.

EVEN BEFORE BLAKE opened the workshop door, he heard the rock music blasting. As he stepped into the room, Spock rushed over to greet him, his black tail wagging. Wes was on his feet, sorting out what looked like junk metal on a work table that had a few gouges and burn marks. Glancing at him, Wes lowered the volume, then grunted a greeting.

"I met your new neighbor at the hardware store." Blake carried in the new paint.

"So did I this morning," Wes said, his attention on the metal pieces, as if he was looking for just the right one.

"She's very attractive."

Wes glanced up, frowning. "A little young for you, isn't she?"

"You're talking about the daughter, right?" Blake chuckled. "I'm talking about the mom."

"Oh." Wes turned back to a piece of rusted metal. "Yeah, I thought you meant the daughter."

"Good." Blake nodded, glad they cleared that up. He didn't want to fight his nephew over a woman. Not that he would fight anyone over a woman. He'd done a lot of stupid things in his life, but not that. Though if there were one woman he'd fight over, Susan might be that one. At least when he'd been younger. At his age now, he'd stand back and wait to see what happened. He'd let the woman choose.

There was silence as he carried planks of reclaimed maple to his worktable in his side of the workroom. Usually he and Wes didn't talk much as they worked on their separate projects. They grunted sometimes and swore other times. Sometimes they stretched and got something to eat or drink from the fridge or the coffeemaker.

Usually, when one stopped for a break, the other stopped, too. They talked about their projects and what they were going to eat. The weather or sports was often a topic. Once in a while, they asked the other for an opinion on their project. Sometimes they asked for help. But for the most part, they had a silent camaraderie.

This silence was different. Blake could feel it simmering, a void waiting to be filled.

Blake had an urge to fill this void. He sat on the workbench chair and swiveled to face Wes. "So, you met the daughter."

"And her baby."

"What do you think about them?"

Wes looked his way. "The baby's cute."

"All babies are cute," Blake said. "Even if you think it's ugly, be smart and lie. Anything else?"

Wes shrugged, the corners of his lips curled up slightly.

Blake smiled slightly, too, before sitting back in his chair. He didn't know what was going to happen here, but he had a feeling it would be interesting. Spring was in the air. The time of year when flowers—and a few body parts—were getting ready to spring up and say *here I come*. Blake was rooting for all things that sprang up.

He took a gulp of coffee, then opened up his laptop and typed in *Susan Perry*.

Immediately the picture of seven women popped up. None looked like the Susan Perry he'd met.

"What's the daughter's last name?" he asked. "Hayley what?"

There was a pause, then Wes said, "Perry."

"She's not married then."

"No."

Blake nodded. "How do you spell her first name? H-A-Y or H-A-I or H-A-L?"

"You think I asked?"

Not replying to Wes's question, Blake typed in *Hailey Perry*. Another seven matches popped up. He opened another page, changed the spelling, and six pictures shot up. There were a couple about the right age. Then he tried *Halley* on another page. That done, he brought the laptop over to Wes. "Any of these look like her?"

Wes glanced at the different pictures for the three spellings. Three times he shook his head.

"Looks like mother and daughter aren't online a lot," Blake said.

"That's my guess. Does it bother you?"

"There's a mystery here," Blake said, "and I've always wanted to solve a mystery. How about you?"

"Me? I just want to mind my own business." Wes stood. "Which reminds me. Ready to go out?" He glanced down at Spock. "Ready to do your business?"

Spock was already on his feet, his mouth open in a happy smile, his eyes on Wes, his tail swiping the air.

Watching Wes and Spock head out of the workshop, Blake shook his head. His nephew was in denial. He was as interested in their neighbor as Blake was interested in the woman's mother. *More* interested than Blake, who'd seen the intensity in his nephew's eyes. Both of those reasons were making it his business, too—his nephew's interest, and his own interest.

Besides, he always did like a mystery.

13

HAYLEY WAS FEEDING THE BABY WHEN HER MOTHER came in with two paint cans and a plastic bag that Hayley guessed held brushes, and a bright smile.

"What a beautiful day," Susan said, a lilt in her voice as she set down the cans on the counter.

"You met a man," Hayley said.

Susan smiled serenely. "I was in a hardware store. Of course I met a man there."

"Wow. Who knew it was easier to pick up a man in a hardware store than a bar?"

"Don't be a grouch. This weather is so refreshing." Susan spread out her arms as if she were going to twirl around. Like a teenager instead of a woman in her fifties.

"And the man?" Hayley asked.

Finn made squeaking sounds. Hayley wiped his face, then pasted a kiss on the side of Finn's forehead and lifted him out of his chair. "Shhh," she said, patting his back. "Everything is good. Grandma's having fun, that's all." She looked at her mother. "You'd better get used to it. This happens a lot with Grandma."

Her mother's face changed, the joy seeping away. "Do you hate it? I don't mean—"

"No! I don't hate it at all, Mom." Hayley sighed. "Maybe I'm just envious. I have Dad's character, and I wish I were more like you."

"I've always loved your father's character," her mother said, her smile back.

Hayley nodded. Her father was the smartest and most responsible men she knew. But it was true she had his character, which was not joyful. Not sexy. She was prudent like him. A planner. She wasn't a seat-of-the-pants person like her mother. She didn't flirt with men in hardware stores. She was cautious before she flirted with anyone.

And look where all that prudence had gotten her. *Stupid, stupid, stupid.*

On paper, Leo had been perfect. A respected businessman who was getting a divorce from his wife. She'd had no idea that his family was the head of a Russian mob. That hadn't popped up on the Internet when she'd punched in his name. She'd had no idea he was pulling some kind of a baby scam. What he'd done was ridiculous. Strange. Unnatural. Most wealthy couples would just find a woman with a similar appearance and pay her to have the husband's baby. There was no reason for the husband to participate. It could all have been done in a doctor's office with the husband's sperm. His penis didn't need to be anywhere near the potential baby mama's vagina.

Susan's fingers snapped, getting her attention. "You're thinking of Leo and his wife."

"It's hard to stop thinking. It makes no sense."

"I've thought about it, too." Susan plopped onto a chair and leaned over the table toward her. "I think the real reason wasn't just your resemblance to his wife. I think Leo wanted the baby to have your brains, your integrity, and your temperament. He wanted a baby that was perfect."

Hayley looked down at the back of Finn's head. He burped, and she realized she'd forgotten to put a towel on her shoulder. With a sigh, she shifted him to her other shoulder, then rubbed his back.

Raising her gaze to her mother, she said, "I owe my integrity and temperament to you as well as to Dad."

"What about your brains?"

"No question there. You know all my brains come from Dad."

Her mother reared back her head and laughed until Hayley joined her. It took a couple minutes for the laughter to die down.

Hayley looked down at Finn, who had fallen asleep while she'd been laughing. "I talked to our next-door neighbor," she said, raising her head.

Her mother leaned toward her again. "Tell me more."

"We just talked. Don't make a big thing out it."

"I'm not saying a word."

"You don't have to say any word. I can tell what you were thinking."

Her mother's smile dipped, and she stared at Hayley, her expression sad.

"What?" Hayley asked. "What now?"

"Don't let what Leo did spoil your life. You have to trust people. If you don't, that means that the creep wins."

"We changed our lives because of him." Conscious of the baby in her arms, Hayley kept her voice low, though she wanted to scream. "We're living in another state under different names because of him."

"And he's in prison. He's paying for what he did."

"His wife was part of it, too. She's not paying for anything. We know it was Leo's idea, and she didn't like it, but she didn't stop him. She could have prevented it."

"Oh, honey, even the strongest woman can sometimes be worn down. Like water dripping on a stone. And since the wife wasn't in contact with you, the Feds couldn't prove her complicity."

"Maybe she was smarter than her husband." Hayley made a face. "Too bad the stupid one had the sperm."

Susan laughed. "And you wouldn't undo Finn, would you?"

Hayley shook her head and ignored an urge to hug him fiercely.

"Then in the end, you won. You have Finn."

"I *won*?" She stared at her mother. "We're not in a bustling city any longer; we're in a nowhere small town."

"A *beautiful* town. A great town. The kind of town where we know our neighbors. How many of your neighbors did you know in Miami?"

"A few." She heard the truculence in her voice.

"Name one."

"Hank and Joan, who lived next door."

"You knew their names because you complained about their yapping dog."

"I *like* dogs, but the little thing was always barking. They left it alone most days and nights."

"Then be happy that you won't have to worry about a barking dog from our new neighbor." Her mother nodded toward the house where her neighbor lived. "His dog isn't a barker. You have to admit that."

"Unlike the man, the dog is well-behaved. It's the man who stared at my breasts like they were his favorite desserts."

Susan laughed. "Sweetie, he's a man. And you do have great breasts. You take after me that way."

"Mom, you are crazy."

"What I am is happy. I have you, and I have my grandson. I'm eager to start something new in my life. I met a handsome man today. I'm *not* going to sit around and mope over a lost life. Instead of looking backward, I'm moving forward." Susan stood, energy vibrating off of her. "I advise you to do the same thing."

Without waiting for Hayley's response, Susan marched out of the kitchen, toward the back of the house.

Finn hit her chest and said, "Ga!"

Looking down at his red curls, Hayley said, "Maybe I did get some of my brains from my mom, too. What do you think?"

Milk dribble came out of Finn's mouth, and she kissed the top of his head. "If I had to do it all over, I would do the same thing in a second. Because now I have you."

Tears suddenly spilled from her eyes, emotion filling her chest and her throat. Her mother was right. Leo and his wife had done the worst thing they could do to her ... and they'd done the best. She needed to let go of her anger and make the best of it. Because the best was right here in her arms.

That didn't mean she would trust another man so quickly. She wasn't ready for that. It might be a long time before she would want that.

Or it might be never.

POLINA SAT ALONE in her chair on the patio, watching the sun go down. Her home was silent. The chef had left. The housekeeper only worked mornings. No one was here. Her friends who used to fawn over her were now avoiding her. She was a pariah. An untouchable.

Since the trial, no one had spoken to her. Everyone blamed her. No one—except perhaps Leo's mother, who knew his faults—believed that the baby scheme had been Leo's idea. They didn't believe she'd begged him to give her time to conceive. They didn't want to believe her. They wanted to blame her.

Her muscles tensed, and she took deep breaths. She needed to stop going over the past. It was done. She had to move on. She had to do what was best for herself now.

Tomorrow she would drive over to the prison and see Leo. Tonight, she would burn inside.

Her phone rang, the sound surprising her.

Looking at the readout, she stiffened, recognizing the caller's name.

Yuri.

Her heart beat heavily inside her chest.

"Yuri," she said, and heard the huskiness in her voice. "Did you find something already?"

"No." There was silence for a moment before he spoke again. "I have a question for you."

"Yes?"

"Does your husband know what you want me to do?"

Her nerves tightened, and so did her grip on the phone. "Why do you ask?"

"Tell me."

More seconds passed before she replied. "No. I didn't tell him, and I don't plan to."

"That's all I need to know."

Her hands shook. She forced herself to speak with a steady tone. "Why do you ask? Will you tell me now?"

"The woman had access to his phone because of Leo's sloppiness. I won't work for someone so stupid."

She closed her eyes for a few seconds before opening them. "Everyone blames me."

"Of course they do. He's the boss's son. That's how life is. Even in prison, he's the one with the power."

"His parents look at me as if they wish me dead. So do his father's men."

"Not all of his men."

"Not you."

"I'm not his man. I'm not his father's man. I'm not his mother's man. I'm my own man."

She swallowed. "I think his family has someone watching my house."

"I'm not surprised."

"If they caught me with another man while Leo's in prison, I think I would soon be dead."

There was silence on the other end. It was suddenly hard for her to breathe, and her heart thumped. She could hear his breaths, slow and even, and the palms of her hands moistened.

"You had your phone checked?" he asked.

"Yes. This is a new phone that I bought after the trial."

"Be careful what you say. You never know for sure."

Then there was silence. He was gone. She knew it. But she waited, in case she was wrong, until finally, just to make sure, she whispered, "Are you there?"

When he didn't reply, she sighed and looked out the window at the darkening sky. She didn't know what she should do. She only knew what she wanted to do, and who she wanted to do it with ... and it wasn't with the appliance in her dresser drawer.

Damn Leo. Damn his mother. Damn his father. Damn the lawyers and the judges and the US Marshal's Witness Protection Program for whisking away the woman and the baby. The baby that she wanted so badly.

The thought was an ache in her chest.

And damn the other woman for being so smart, so self-reliant. So much wiser than Leo. So much wiser than her.

She opened one of the patio doors. Still holding her phone, she stepped onto the patio and to the edge, where she gazed down at the ocean below.

It would be so easy to fall. To lean over the thigh-high railing and tumble down.

She continued to peer down for a long moment, then stepped back, her spine straight, her muscles tensed, her teeth clenched.

Not her. Never her. Someone else might give up, but she was a fighter. A survivor. She would find a way out of this.

She wanted to call Yuri again. Looking down, she saw that the cell phone was shaking.

No, not the phone. Her hand.

She dropped the phone, hearing it crack on the patio floor. She looked down at it, her mouth open. She didn't know why her hand was shaking so much. She always had such iron control.

This whole fiasco was Leo's fault. The jury had thought the woman was the victim, but what they didn't know was that the one suffering was her. The woman had the baby. *She* was the one left with nothing at all.

Her hands curled into fists. She raised them, then brought them down hard on the railing. So hard it hurt. But she raised them again. Slammed them down on the railing again. Then again. And again. And again. Until her knuckles bled and she fell on her knees. With tears running down her face, she laid her head down on the concrete patio floor and cried with gulping sobs as angry thoughts whirled in circles in her head, and only four of them were coherent.

She wasn't the bad person in this.

She would find the baby.

She would take it back.

They would all be sorry.

14

HAYLEY CAREFULLY SAT DOWN ON THE FORMERLY UGLY brown recliner that, twenty-eight hours since her mother had painted it, was now a light minty green.

"Here goes." Susan plopped onto the matching recliner.

They both chair-danced with their butts for about two minutes. Hayley was wearing light gray slacks. Susan had on white slacks. Susan jumped up first and stood with her back to Hayley, looking over her shoulder. "See any green?"

"Not a speck."

"Good." Susan turned around and stepped back. "Let me see yours."

Hayley jumped up, laughing. She remembered making making faces on cookies with her mother when she was a child, using white frosting and chocolate chips. Painting recliners reminded her of those days.

She turned her back to Susan, who clapped her hands. "It worked! Our butts have no paint on them, and the recliners look beautiful."

Hayley stepped back to get a view of both of the recliners, and she had to agree.

"I've changed my mind," her mother said.

"You don't like the green?"

"No, I don't like the color. I *love* the color. I loved painting them. Looking at them makes me happy. I feel so proud." She sucked in a deep breath and held out her arms, like a bird spreading its wings. "*This* is what I want to do. It's much more creative and satisfying than staging homes. I just took something ugly and I made it beautiful. How amazing is that?"

Hayley turned, her stomach tight. She'd been through so many changes in this last year and a half. Not little changes but huge, life-altering changes.

She reminded herself that she wasn't the only one who'd gone through changes. Her mother had gone through everything with her. She'd even been at her side as she was giving birth.

Her mother had left Miami for her.

Now it was her turn to support her mom.

"That's a wonderful idea. You'll be great at it."

Her mom laughed, hugged her tightly, then stepped back and put her hands on Hayley's shoulders. "I knew you'd hate it."

"*Hate* is an ugly word." She heard the wobble in her voice as she forced her lips up into a smile. "That's what you used to tell me. Remember?"

Susan nodded, her eyes moistening.

"Painting furniture wouldn't be anything that I'm good at doing," Hayley said, "but *you* are creative. It's what you want to do, so you should do it."

Susan sniffed. "I know you sometimes wondered why I never married."

"Because you weren't madly in love. That's what you told me."

"I said that?" Susan made a face. "I lied. I was madly in love often, but I found that the madness usually cooled. Do you know why it cooled?"

"Not really."

"Because every time I've been in a serious relationship, the man wants me to change. They're all like that. Every. Single. Time. They wanted me to watch them play their games, but they were never interested in my hobbies. My dancing. My book clubs. Or the time I joined a choir and sang at different churches."

Hayley winced. Her mother loved singing, but singing didn't love her.

"What men really wanted," Susan continued, "was for me to be there for them with dinner waiting. They certainly didn't want me showing houses in the evening and on weekends."

"Was Dad like that?" Hayley asked.

"Oh, honey." Susan shook her head. "Your dad was the best. He and I knew early on that we were opposites. I loved his intelligence and his droll humor and his honesty. He loved my laughter and my enjoyment of life. But we didn't fit together. We didn't have any conflicts because we both knew that."

Hayley sighed. "I knew that, too. You're one side of a coin, and he's the other. Anyway, I think you should do this."

"I have an idea. Remember I told you I met a man in the hardware store? And he helped me with my purchases?"

"Yes?" Hayley made herself smile. She wasn't going to bring her mother down. She wasn't going to disapprove of everything her beautiful and fun mother did or said. After all, they were here instead of in Miami because *she* had been the one who'd chosen badly, not her mother.

"I didn't want to say this earlier," Susan said. "I didn't want to upset you. But the hardware man is our next door neighbor's uncle."

Hayley sighed and then laughed. There had to be a God. One who had a warped sense of humor and liked to play tricks on humans. "It's okay, Mom. Honest, I'm fine with that."

"You don't mind? Really?"

"Of course I don't mind. Our neighbor isn't the enemy, though he did stare at my breasts."

"He's a man." Her mother shrugged. "It's hard for them not to look."

"That's such a bad excuse, but I talked to him yesterday—maybe about the same time you were enchanting his uncle—"

Her mother laughed.

Hayley grinned. "Our neighbor and I are okay now. I'll have to be more careful with the blinds. I'm just not used to a *real* next-door neighbor. One I actually talk to. It's so different here from Miami."

Her mother's eyebrows rose. "Next you'll be saying he's kind of cute."

"Well, he is kind of cute."

Her mother's eyebrows rose higher.

Hayley shook her head. "I know what you're thinking, and it's not that. You raised me to not need a man, and everything that happened this last year just reinforced it." She looked out the window. The retired fifth-grade teacher across the street was walking her dog. Hayley couldn't remember the former teacher's name, but the big reddish dog was Rusty.

"You're smiling," Susan said. "Good. Then you won't mind if I invite Blake and his nephew to dinner."

"A *double* date?"

"Not a date. It's my way of thanking Blake for helping me. And since his nephew lives next door, it would be rude if we didn't invite him, too."

"Rude. Right."

Her mother beamed at her. "Then you won't mind?"

"I won't mind. I just don't want you to think that I'm ready for romance. Far from it. I'm a new mom, after all." She cupped her breasts. "And right now these breasts aren't made for loving. They're made for breakfast, lunch, dinner, and the occasional snack."

Her mother laughed, then patted her shoulder. "I'll set it up. It's just dinner. Nothing more. No hookup. We're being sociable with our neighbors. It will be good for you."

"Like a spoonful of medicine?"

Her mother's laugh was low. At the same time, a loud cry came from the bedroom, where Finn had been napping.

Hayley turned. Butterflies fluttered their wings inside her chest. "Fine. We're having dinner with our neighbors. Now I have to feed Finn."

She stepped away because nothing was as important to her right now as Finn. No one needed her as much as he did. She didn't suppose that anyone would ever need her more. Especially not a man.

WES WAS SCRUBBING the rust off of an old pipe he was using for a lamp stand when Blake's cell phone buzzed. At his worktable, he put the phone to his ear and leaned back. Wes watched from his side of the workroom. Something was going on. Blake had sparked up. He was half smiling, his eyes lidded. Then he grinned widely and said something. He reminded Blake of a teenager talking to a new girlfriend.

Wes switched his gaze to the pipe. Who Blake talked to was none of his business, though he guessed who was putting that syrupy smile on his uncle's face. He'd seen the lady, and he felt a little syrupy himself about the lady's daughter. His problem was that the daughter had a child, though apparently there was no man in the picture. That was fine with Wes, but something seemed to be off about their situation.

There certainly was nothing off about Hayley. Everything about her had looked just right to him. But looks lied. When she spoke about herself, she held herself tightly, afraid to let go, afraid to loosen up.

He knew what that was like. He held himself tightly, too, not letting anyone in. Not even his uncle, even though he was doing okay now. He had his dog. He could walk. And he wasn't falling apart at every loud noise. He'd even found something that he enjoyed doing. A psychiatrist might even say there was a connection to the lights he created and the light he wanted to see in the world.

But he didn't need a psychiatrist. He was one of the lucky ones. Thanks to his dog, his uncle, and the VA Health Care, he was healing mentally and physically. Damaged but functioning.

When he talked to Hayley, he could see that she was damaged, too. Not physically. Emotionally.

What had damaged her? *Who* had damaged her?

Blake laughed and turned toward him. "I'll tell Wes. Sure, we'll both be there. Six o'clock sounds good. I'll bring something to drink. What's your favorite?"

Spock, who'd been lying on the padded rug on the floor, made a grunting noise and got up to his feet. Probably feeling Wes's unrest.

Wes switched his gaze back to his grinning uncle. Only a woman could have put that big smile on his face. In another couple of minutes, Blake would be drooling like a horny teenager.

Spock stepped over to Wes, nudging his hand. Not taking his gaze from his uncle, Wes petted Spock's smooth head. The satiny fur against his palm and fingers calmed him.

Still talking on the phone, Blake belted out a laugh, then said, "We'll be looking forward to it. See you tonight."

As if in slow motion, Blake set down his cell phone and straightened from his teenage slouch. "We're going to dinner tonight with two beautiful women."

"We?"

"You and me."

Wes didn't say anything. Just watched him.

"It's your neighbor and her mother."

"I guessed that's what you meant. I don't recall being asked if I wanted to go."

"And I don't recall," Blake drawled, "that you had a stick up your ass. If you don't want to go, then don't. I'm not your social secretary. I thought you liked the daughter. I guess I was wrong."

Wes's chest felt tight. Constricted. In his mind, he saw her breasts again. He swallowed. They were just breasts. Like she'd said, the purpose of breasts was to feed babies, not to titillate a man. After all, he had breasts, too. Two ineffective male breasts. And he'd seen a few male breasts that were bigger than some women's. Not a pretty sight.

"I can see you thinking," his uncle said. "Spit it out."

"I'm an idiot," Wes said.

"You won't get any argument from me."

"You like her mother, don't you?"

"Sure." Blake nodded. "But I've liked women before. I don't need you as my wingman. If you don't want to go, I'll find someone else."

"I'll go."

"Will you try to lighten up a little?" Blake asked.

"You want me to be the life of the party?"

"Not sure that I can believe in a miracle as big as that. So, what do you think we should bring? Beer? Wine?"

"Wine sounds good." Wes reached for his computer. Because he had an idea…

15

THE DOORBELL RANG. HAYLEY REMAINED IN THE LIVING room, relaxing on the newly painted recliner, as her mother let the two men in and thanked Blake for his bottle of wine, saying something that made them laugh. Hayley laughed, too, under her breath. Her mother was doing it again, enchanting a man with her laughter and vivaciousness.

There was a spring of joy inside her mother that Hayley didn't have—nor anyone else that Hayley knew. Yet women liked her mother as well as men. She spread happiness. There weren't enough people like her.

Certainly not Hayley, but that was okay with her. She was the lucky one, having Susan for her mom.

Finn, in his bouncy infant seat, sobbed once, then quieted. Hayley wasn't sure if the sob was because of the company or if Finn sensed her nervousness. She exhaled slowly, reminding herself that she'd testified against the son of a Russian Mafia boss in court ten days after she'd given birth to Finn. If she could do that, she could do *this*. It wasn't as if she were a flat-chested teenager again just beginning to date. In fact, she had breasts right now that a porn star would envy, a short-term benefit of giving birth.

And one of the two men in the house had seen them.

She pushed up off the chair and forced a smile as Wes headed toward her.

"Hi," Wes said.

"Hi."

A few feet behind him, her mother put her hand over her mouth to hide a smile. Wes's uncle Blake rolled his eyes.

Really? They were acting as if she and Wes were teenagers.

Wes held out a brown paper bag to her. "This is for Finn."

She took the bag and opened it. Inside it was something encased in plastic and metal with small bulbs. "Is it a light?"

"Lights, plural." He pulled a fixture out of the bag. It opened up into a three-foot circle.

"Gah!" Finn called. "Gah!"

Wes smiled at Finn, then turned to Hayley. "This attaches to the top of a bassinet or a crib. All you need to do is screw the clamps in."

"I'm sure I can do that," she said.

"It has blue and purple lights. Babies are attracted to blue and purple."

"I didn't know that. This is magical. Did you make this?"

He nodded and ducked his head slightly. "It has a small motor, so the lights will circle around, and it has three different speeds."

"Wow, that's ... brilliant. And so thoughtful. Finn will love it. Thank you. Do you, um, have a diagram on where to put the clamps?"

"I'll set it up." He turned toward the hall without asking where it was.

Because he knew exactly where it was, she thought as she scooped Finn out of his seat and hurried after him.

"You don't have to do it. I'll figure it out."

He didn't reply, he just kept on going.

She wanted to stick her tongue out at him, but that would have been childish. Besides, she was the same way. It was easier to do something herself instead of explaining.

He set the light fixture up in a few minutes. The sunlight shone through the blue and purple lights, giving them a sparkle even before he pressed a switch and the lights brightened. She put Finn in the bassinet. His eyes followed the lights, his mouth open wide, pure awe in his face. A happy sound came out of his throat, and his arms slashed up toward the lights, trying to touch them but they were out of his reach.

"Oooh." Hayley twirled around to Wes. He was watching her, as if she was the reason he'd brought the lights. Not Finn.

She laughed, feeling carefree and ... something else. *Happy.* That was it.

Then she shivered and stopped smiling. Afraid of the emotion. Her heart beating too fast as he stared into her eyes.

He turned away first, looking at Finn, who was waving his arms and gurgling.

"The baby likes it," he said.

"Yes." Her voice sounded strangled to her own ears. "Yes."

They stood in the room for another moment, looking down at Finn, and she felt the warmth coming from this man standing only a few inches from her. She felt his solidity. She felt his presence.

Two pairs of footsteps came from the hall. Her mother and Finn's uncle. Hayley shuffled sideways, a couple feet away from Wes.

He did the same thing, so they were standing on opposite ends of the bassinet, like two shy teenagers.

Then her mom and his uncle were in the room, and she and Wes stepped farther away from the bassinet to allow the two to exclaim over the lights.

She looked at Wes on the other side of the bassinet, and he looked at her.

Thank you, she mouthed. A congestion in her chest wouldn't let her speak aloud. This was so … uncomfortable. Standing across from this man who had made this beautiful gift. He'd done this for her. To impress her. If that had been his goal, he'd definitely succeeded.

She stepped toward the hallway as her mom and his uncle remained by the bassinet, still admiring the lights. She glanced back.

Wes was following her.

She had known he would. The thought let her breathe normally. He liked her. She liked him. And, really, there was nothing wrong with that.

"Where's your dog?" she asked.

"My uncle thought I should leave Spock at home in case he makes you or your mom uncomfortable."

"You know I like Spock. My mother likes dogs, too."

"That's what I thought but..." He shrugged. "Uncle Blake knows more about women than I do. He's been married twice."

"Really? How did that work out?"

His lips curved up. "Not so well."

She grinned. "Next time trust your own instincts. I bet you're missing Spock."

"I've gotten used to having him by my side."

"He's probably missing you, too. Why don't you go and bring him over?"

His uncle's laughter came from the bedroom, along with the brighter tones of laughter from her mother.

"I'll do that." He stepped sideways, the move awkward for him.

Her instinct was to reach out to steady him, but she remained still as he caught his balance. "I'll come with you."

"I don't need help."

"It's beautiful outside, and I'd like a short walk without Finn for once. Don't make a big thing about it. After all, you've been peeking into my bedroom since before we met."

His lips curved up. "Are you ever going to forget that?"

"No." She held back a laugh.

"Neither will I." He looked at her for a moment, then slowly turned and stepped back into the bedroom. Hayley followed him.

"I'm going to get Spock," he said, his voice projecting to his uncle and her mom, who were chatting in low voices over the bassinet.

His uncle's eyebrows went up.

"It was my idea," Hayley said. "I'll walk over to his house, too. Will you watch—"

"Go." Her mom made a shooing motion with her hands. "Go."

Wes was already heading away. Hayley followed him down the hall and out of the house. He walked steadily if not fast, stepping on the sidewalk instead of the lawn. She suspected the lawn wasn't as level. The sun wasn't shining as brightly as when they'd come in, and a slight chill in the air made her shiver.

"Cold?" he asked.

"Just a little. I'm not used—" She stopped the words that wanted to come out of her mouth, *used to this weather*. Their background story was that they'd lived in Chicago, and Chicago natives were not strangers to cold weather.

"Used to what?" he asked.

"Um, nothing. Here's your house." She gestured.

He looked sideways at her, a small smile on his face. "Thanks for letting me know."

"Anytime."

He chuckled. As they headed up the sidewalk, an excited *woof* came from inside the house.

"Someone's happy to see you," she said.

"Spock. I was lucky to get him. He's the best."

They reached the front porch, and he stepped up without needing any help. Instead of opening the door, he turned to her. "You said that before we met, it was your house I was peeking at."

Her eyebrows arched. "You really want to go there?"

Laughter sparkled in his eyes.

"Go on." She shook her head. "Say it. Get this over with."

He grinned. "Just wanted to make it clear that it wasn't your house that made me stand and stare and feel like a teenage boy all over again."

A sharp bark came from inside the house, and she laughed. "Are you happy now that you've gotten that out of your mouth?"

"Actually, I am."

She socked his upper left arm. He chuckled, then opened the door, stepped inside, and greeted Spock. The black dog whined with happiness, as if Wes had been gone for twenty days instead of twenty minutes.

There was just enough room for her to squeeze in, the screen door banging shut behind her. She knew that in her position, her mother would be looking around the room, but Hayley kept her gaze on the man and the dog.

Still petting the dog, Wes peered up at her. "Does this mean we're friends now?"

"I suppose it does. Life is strange, isn't it?"

He looked at her for a long moment, not replying, still half-bent over Spock, the black dog's whole body vibrating with excitement, his mouth open in a large doggy smile.

Straightening, Wes turned to the screen door and nodded at Spock, who immediately went into position next to him. She stepped out the door ahead of Wes. He had his dog. He hadn't needed her on the walk over, and he certainly didn't need her now.

"You're right," he said as they turned down the sidewalk to her place. "Life is strange. Sometimes it feels like hell. Other times it feels like heaven."

She stopped and turned toward him. "What are you saying?"

He stopped, too. "I like you. But I should warn you that I'm damaged."

"We're all damaged." Her voice was steady, but she was shaking inside.

He took a deep breath. "I'm attracted to you."

"I know."

"Am I wrong to think that the attraction is mutual?"

"It is, but I had a bad breakup." She made a face. "A *really* bad breakup. I'm not sure—"

"I'm not your ex."

"I know. It's just—"

"And I'm not talking about anything permanent."

Her eyebrows rose. "You're full of romance, aren't you? A real sweet talker."

He groaned. "I didn't mean—"

"I'm not taking offense. You're being honest, even when it makes you look bad. I can't tell you how much I appreciate that. So much that I'm actually enjoying this conversation."

They turned toward her house. "It's not much of a conversation. Just me making an ass of myself."

"I'm getting used to that."

"I should keep my mouth shut," he said.

She gripped his upper arm, stopping him. "It's a little late for that. For both of us. You may as well tell me what you're thinking."

He looked at her for a long moment, and her heart beat faster as he stared at her, his eyes wary. "It's been a long time since I've been with a woman."

"It's been over a year for me since I've had sex," she said.

"More than two years for me."

"Your body was damaged."

"I'm better now. And since the first time I saw you… Well, it's my leg that's damaged. Everything else is working."

"I'm glad for you, but that's a little more than I need to know."

He groaned. "I'm making a mess of this."

Laughter was bubbling up inside of her. She liked his awkwardness. It made her want to put her hand on his arm. Step even closer to him.

"Go on," she said.

"I don't know how to do this anymore."

"It's not that hard. You open your mouth and say what you think."

"If I say what I think, I might get slapped in the face."

"Say it." She held her head high. "I dare you."

He stared at her, a slight frown on his face. The dog stared at her, too, his mouth open, looking happy.

"I won't slap you," she said.

"I hope not. Spock might try to protect me."

"In that case, you have nothing to worry about except looking foolish. And I'm the queen of looking foolish."

He was silent for a long moment. "You're sure?"

"I'm sure that you're stalling. If you want something, ask for it."

His gaze steady on her face, he said, "I'd like to have sex with you. I can't promise anything permanent, but I don't have any diseases. I'm not kinky. I'm not mean. I'm not—"

"Stop!" She held up her hand. "We're not in love, and we don't know each other well. Don't tell me why I *shouldn't* have unromantic sex with you. Tell me why I *should.*"

He frowned. "You want me to sell myself?"

She had to hold back from rolling her eyes. Didn't he get it? Didn't he know? Selling themselves was what every guy and every girl did when they dated. They used the best packaging and said the best words. They tried to look shiny. They…

She stopped. Wes wasn't doing any of those things.

Neither was she. She was a breastfeeding mom who'd come out of one of the world's worst relationships. A relationship so strange that she couldn't even call it a relationship. And she didn't feel like flirting. She didn't want to impress Wes. All she wanted from him was … well, she wasn't sure if she did want anything.

But why shouldn't she have sex with him? She enjoyed sex. Why let Leo ruin that for her?

"Sell myself." He frowned. "To start with, I won't do anything you don't like. I'll treat you well. I won't lie to you. I'll—"

She held up her arm, stopping him. "You mean it? You're not lying to me?"

"I meant everything I said."

She put her hand over her heart that was beating too hard. He wasn't even trying to be romantic. He was telling her up front how he felt.

"I like your honesty," she said. "I'm not physically damaged. I'm not even allowing myself to be emotionally damaged. That would give other people too much power, and no one has that power over me. What I will say I am is bruised. Emotionally bruised."

His eyes stared into hers. "I've never hurt a woman, and I won't start with you."

She stared back at him for another long moment. She should say no. She'd been trying to make the best of an insane situation for the last year, but inwardly she'd been so angry. Now the anger was slowly seeping away. Now she felt ready to dip her toe into life again. And not just life with her mother and her son. A part of life that she hadn't expected to experience again for a long time.

Why should she be deprived of one of the joys of life?

And this man who'd been damaged while he was serving his country… Didn't he deserve joy, too?

"There's an old Marvin Gaye song called 'Sexual Healing,'" she said. "Maybe we both need some sexual healing."

His brown eyes darkened and seemed to burn hot. She gulped and turned toward her temporary home, and so did he. The two-minute walk felt like twenty minutes as she wondered with each step what she'd just agreed to do. Just before they reached the door, he took her hand in his and stopped. So did she. So did Spock.

"You're sure?" he asked.

She looked down at his hand that was holding hers. Funny how it felt good. She liked his grip. Not too hard. Not too soft. It was just right.

She wondered if the way he held her hand would be similar to his lovemaking. Not too soft. Not too hard. Not too gentle. Not too rough. Not too short. Not too long.

Someone was breathing hard, and it took a couple seconds to realize that she was the heavy breather. She inhaled sharply and looked up at him. "Yes. I'm very sure."

"When?"

"I'm free almost anytime. You tell me, and we'll figure it out."

"I'll call you," he said.

She nodded and drew her hand from his. They turned back to the house. She couldn't tell him she'd have to talk it over with her mother. In case she needed a babysitter.

As they went into the house, she was holding back her laughter.

This was a strange new life. She might as well enjoy it—in every way possible.

16

"*It's important. Come alone.*" The four words in Yuri's voice, husky and seductive, repeated in Polina's mind, giving her a thousand jaded thoughts as she drove to his upper eastside home.

Perhaps she was paranoid, but before turning into Yuri's driveway, she glanced behind her. No one slowed. If anyone had been following her, she must have lost them in the congested traffic crawl a couple of miles ago.

She parked, then stepped out of the car. The sky was dusky, the air warm and humid. She heard music from down the block, a Cuban dance beat. She breathed in the humid air that tasted like sex, then glanced down at her purple dress that fit the music and her mood. Purple was a strong color, and tonight she wanted to be strong. She'd been weak for too long.

She switched her gaze to Yuri's house. It was a traditional home, with stucco walls and red clay roof tiles, the style so different from the sleek, modern design of her oceanfront home that had been featured in three different magazines.

A house that felt as sterile as she was. Hot and shiny on the outside and cold and barren on the inside.

Pushing away her thoughts, she headed to the front door. With every step, her heart pounded a little too hard and a little too fast.

The door opened before she had a chance to press the doorbell. Yuri stood in the doorway. He wore a blue T-shirt and black slacks, yet he looked masculine and sophisticated. And sexy. He reeked of testosterone, so much that she thought he should have big letters on his T-shirt saying DANGER: THIS MAN IS ON FIRE.

"That was fast," she said.

He gestured for her to step inside. "I was expecting you. You're punctual."

She strode past him. This Miami neighborhood was not for the poor, nor for the very rich. It was somewhere in between.

"This is ... nice." She stopped in the middle of the front room and looked around at the cream-colored walls, the high ceilings and open floor plan, the gold and brown Spanish-styled furniture with red and royal blue accents. She turned to him. "Very welcoming. Did you choose the colors and style yourself?"

"A designer helped me, but if you're asking whether I live here with a woman, the answer is no."

"If I was curious about your living arrangements, I would have asked."

He smiled slightly.

She pressed her lips together. So what if she wanted to know if he were involved with a woman? So what if his answer relieved her? She was a woman of passion, but she was also a woman with brains. She wasn't going to do anything that would jeopardize her standing or her life.

If her in-laws suspected she was cheating with another man, she doubted she would live long. In their community, men could cheat with impunity, but women who did the same thing were whores.

"I'll show you the house," he said.

She nodded, and he strode ahead to take her on a tour of the downstairs. The house had an open plan, the mature palm trees in the front yard giving him privacy. The living room opened up to the dining room, which opened up to the kitchen and, on the other side of the kitchen, a great room with furniture that looked big enough to sink into. The kind of furniture her father would have liked if her mother would have allowed it. The kind that Polina would have liked, too.

Then there was a large glass window in the back with a view to the yard that she guessed was bigger than most in the area. The pièce de résistance was a swimming pool.

Looking at this house and backyard made her heart squeeze. Her home was a showpiece. His was ... comfortable. A safe place.

A family place.

"Something wrong?" he asked.

"Your house feels like a home."

"It is my home. Do you want to see the second floor?"

"The bedrooms?" Her eyes narrowed. "No."

The corners of his lips slanted up with amusement. He gestured toward the kitchen. "Ready for dinner?"

"This isn't a date."

"I never said it was. But you're here, and I haven't eaten. If you haven't eaten yet, you may as well join me."

As she turned to say something sharp, she realized she was hungry. Starving. "I'd like that. Thank you."

"Then come to the table. We'll eat first, talk after." He turned.

She followed, admitting to herself that it was pleasant to dine with someone. Since Leo's conviction, she'd felt isolated. Even before that. While he'd been romancing another woman, he'd been living in his penthouse. During those horrible weeks, she'd mostly associated with women she didn't care about and who didn't care about her. The other mob wives, who lived to show off their skimpy designer gowns and their jewelry and their big houses. The bigger and the shinier, the better.

Most of them with children of different ages.

By then, she'd known it was possible that it might never happen to them.

She'd known that if Leo hadn't been so enamored of her, he would have discarded her. That he chose a woman who was a pale replica of her was a testament to his desire for her. Or rather, a testament to her looks. Since her teen years, boys and men had stopped and stared at her, and women had glared.

"You're going far," her mother had told her. "Make sure you don't give it away. Don't go for the pretty men. Go for the rich ones. Promise me."

She'd promised. On her wedding day, she'd held her head up proudly. She'd made it. She'd married the man of her mother's dreams.

But now her dream was in tatters, and she wanted more than her mother's dream. She wanted the baby that Leo had created. Because what if Leo had been right? What if she couldn't conceive?

And if she did have the baby, everything would be all right again.

When she held the baby in her arms, *she* would be in control.

So she sat and waited and watched Yuri use the grill in his kitchen—because the bugs were out in force tonight—and she told herself that maybe she would sleep with Yuri, because why not? Why not be like a man? Why not have it all? Sex. Money. Power.

Why not? Why the hell not?

As long as no one who knew her found out.

The sky darkened as they ate their dinner and talked about plays and movies and music that they liked. The coldness that he'd displayed before this had mellowed. Maybe because they were in his home. Or maybe it had been her all along. Maybe she saw coldness because there had been ice in her heart.

And day by day, it felt to her that the ice was melting.

She wasn't surprised that they liked the same music. Slow and sexy Cuban music that heated her body from her head to her toes. Leo liked pop music, though she suspected he had a tin ear and only liked music sung by the women who wore the least clothes and were on page one of the tabloids. Women who were beautiful and exuded sex.

Like her. She was still the most beautiful. The sexiest.

But by the time he was out of the jail, she wouldn't be the most beautiful. She was twenty-seven now. At her peak. But even a few years would take the gloss out of her complexion. Her body would change, her breasts would droop slightly lower.

But Leo... As long as his father was alive and in charge, Leo would still be powerful. And when you were powerful, it didn't matter what you looked like or how you treated others. Even the bride you had sworn to love and worship.

He just needed to get out of prison before his father's reign was over. Right now, his father appeared to be in great health, fit and energetic. But he was in his late fifties. He could live for decades yet, healthy and virile, making his own new babies.

Or he could die of an aneurysm or cancer or a car accident.

Or a bullet.

Anything could happen.

"How is Leo?" Yuri asked. "I heard the lawyers are working on appeals."

"The lawyers are being paid money, so of course they're doing all they can, even if they know they don't stand a chance in hell."

"Lawyers. Sharks. Politicians." He shrugged.

"Hurricanes," she said. "Natural disasters. Mosquitoes."

He snorted. "We could go on, but it would ruin our appetite. Let's not talk about the reason you're here until after dinner. Right now I'm eating good food with a beautiful woman, and that's what I want to concentrate on."

She nodded and continued to eat, small bites, some of her joy diminished. Oddly because of his words and her own thoughts about her looks. *Right now I'm eating good food with a beautiful woman...*

Right now was the accurate phrase. Beauty wouldn't last forever.

One reason she needed the baby in her arms. Leo's baby would keep her rolling in the money. Their baby would return her power.

And she'd be a good mother. A wonderful mother. She would love the baby so much that the baby would have to love her back.

She finished her dinner but refused seconds and shook her head at the key lime pie. He didn't have seconds, but he ate the pie. She waited for him to finish and then clear the table. When he sat down, she refused another glass of wine.

"I have to drive home," she said.

"You could stay here tonight."

She raised her eyebrows. "You have relevant news? Or are you wasting my time?"

"If you insist..." He leaned back. "One of the marshals has a child who needs a kidney. She'll do anything for a transplant. Her son is on an organ waiting list, but he has a rare blood type. AB minus. If she can get a healthy kidney that will be a match, she'll give you the information."

"Find a healthy kidney for her child? That's insane."

"Some people would think what you want is insane."

Her eyes narrowed and she stiffened. "Go on. What will I need to do?"

"It won't be easy. Or cheap. If you're serious about this, that's my only answer. If you can't do this, perhaps you aren't motivated enough for me to waste *my* time."

"Tell me." Leaning toward him, she repeated, "*Tell me*."

"The kid's father is a bum. The AB minus blood type came from the ex. He's had trouble with drugs, and he's ruled out as a donor. But he has two older kids by another woman. The boy's mother called the kids' mother and found out the eighteen-year-old has AB blood type."

"I would like to think that the second mother agreed, but if she did say yes already, you wouldn't be talking to me about it."

"You're a smart woman. The mother doesn't want her son to do it. The marshal offered her money, but the boy's mother said it wasn't enough. The marshal thinks if we pay the mother enough money, she'll change her mind."

"We could just talk to the kid. At eighteen, he could make his own decision."

"The marshal tried several times to contact him, but he's not replying. She has no choice but to deal with the mom. She's afraid if she keeps trying to contact the kid herself, she'll alienate her son's half brother and they won't have a chance."

She stared at him for a long moment. "You're saying that this might be our only chance to find the baby, right?"

"I'm not saying anything like that. I'm not God."

"*No one* would ever mistake you for God."

"What would they mistake me for?"

"The devil. And stop flirting."

He grinned, then grew serious. "The marshal said the woman is greedy, but she can't talk to the woman anymore. She's afraid she'll say something in anger, and her son will never get the kidney."

"She wants you to do the dirty work."

"That's why you're paying me. If you agree, I'll take over the bargaining."

"How much do you think she'll need?"

"You could give a limit of two hundred thousand."

"She'll come back to you with three hundred thousand."

"Or more," he said. "I could put her off two or three days, but the marshal wants it settled as soon as possible. Every day matters."

"Tell her two hundred fifty thousand. If that's not enough, I'll go up to three hundred thousand."

"What if she still asks for more?"

"Tell her the person you're representing doesn't have that much money. Tell her that three hundred thousand will pretty much wipe me out."

"Is that your last offer? Your best offer?"

"Will it be enough?" she asked.

"I believe it will."

She stood. "Then go with that."

He stood, too. "Are you leaving?"

"Not right now. I'm going to have sex with you, and then I'll leave." She gestured toward the stairway. "Is your bedroom upstairs?"

His eyes burned. "Yes."

She strode to the stairway, her heart beating fast.

She could be killed for this.

But she kept her head up, and she kept walking...

17

WES AND BLAKE WERE GONE. FINN, WHO HAD BEEN napping in his bedroom, had awoken, wet and smelly and hungry and loud. That had been the signal for the men to stand and say it was time to leave. Spock stood, too, breathing hard and gazing at Hayley with a happy smile. Probably smelling the breast milk that was starting to leak out of her nipples.

At the doorway, Wes had paused and looked at her, then shrugged, the early night sky a dark blue behind him. She'd shaken her head, laughed, and then hurried to Finn.

She returned to the kitchen twenty minutes later, holding her satisfied son in her arms while her mother finished loading up the dishwasher, closed the door, pressed the start button, then grabbed the bottle of wine on the counter and held it up.

"Another glass?" Susan asked.

Hayley shook her head. She'd read that two glasses of wine were probably all right for a breastfeeding mother, but she stuck to one glass. Even before her pregnancy, she'd normally stick to one glass.

Every once in a while, she still wondered how this had happened to her, the straightest, most boring woman in the world.

"I thought you'd say that," her mother said. "I prepared your special nursing tea."

Hayley grimaced. She was so predictable.

Her mother carried Hayley's mug and her wineglass into the living room. Hayley trailed her. After setting down the drinks on the small table between the two repainted recliners, Susan held out her arms. "Let me snuggle with my favorite boyfriend."

In a minute, they were sitting in the recliners they'd shown off to the two men. As if that was the real reason they'd gotten together, and it had nothing to do with her mother and Wes's uncle having trouble taking their eyes off of each other.

Hayley sipped her tea, then set it down and closed her eyes as her mother made silly baby talk. Finn laughed and clapped his fish-like hands. Hayley opened her eyes to watch them. Now he was slapping her mother's arm, his smiling face tilted up at her.

He loved his grandmother. He loved his mother.

It hurt Hayley to think that his grandfather couldn't see him like this. Her father was another victim of Leo's twisted scheming. Someday she and Finn would sneak away and meet her father in a safe place, but that day probably wouldn't be for at least a couple of years.

"You and Wes looked pretty cozy tonight," her mother said.

Hayley snorted. "If anyone was cozy, it was you and Blake."

Her mother laughed. "Blake seems like a great guy. Very sexy."

"Aren't there things that a mother shouldn't share with her daughter?"

"Normally, I don't." Susan sighed. "But normally I'm not living with you."

Hayley winced. "I know. You've uprooted your life because of me. I shouldn't complain."

"We're not complaining, we're adjusting. We're making the best of this new life. *Both* of us." Susan grinned. "And I could see sparks between you and Wes."

"You need to make an appointment with an optometrist. Your eyes need to be checked."

"Maybe *you* should get some birth control." The laughter faded from her mother's face. "This time it will be real birth control and not fake pills."

Hayley felt a savage bolt of anger at Leo, and she was glad her mother was holding Finn. He would feel her anger, and it would upset him. She grabbed the mug of tea, took a sip to calm her fast-beating heart, then said, "I made an appointment with a doctor in Sturgeon Bay."

"Birth control?"

She nodded.

"So!" Her mother's voice was triumphant, and Finn made a similar sound that ended in a squeak. "You *are* planning on getting together with Wes."

Hayley groaned and put her hand on her forehead. "Mom, I don't feel comfortable talking to you about this. And it's a little creepy that you're so happy that your daughter might have sex in the near future."

"Honey." Her mother's voice was stricken. "I didn't mean to make you feel awkward. I never thought—"

"I know. You're not only my mom, you're my best friend. But some things are weird."

"I was actually about to say something very motherly."

Hayley slumped back in the chair. "Sorry. Go ahead. I'd love to hear something motherly."

"Gah!" Finn said, his hands flying up. Susan bent over him, talking softly while Finn laughed, then cuddled up on her breast, his eyes closing. Looking so cute and lovable that it was an ache in Hayley's heart.

Despite the way Finn's father had tricked her into pregnancy, she wasn't sorry for Finn's birth. It turned out that he was the real love of her life—the same thing her mother often said about her.

Maybe she was more like her mom than she'd thought.

"These two men," her mother said as Finn snuggled in her arms, "Wes and Blake, are valued in this small community."

Finn made a whining sound, and Susan soothed him.

Hayley waited for Finn's eyes to close before speaking. "Because of their skills?" she asked.

Her mother laughed softly. "You're so smart about some things but so clueless about men."

"I know I'm stupid about men. That's the reason we're here, isn't it?"

"That's *not* what I meant. I just wanted to point out that well-liked and attractive single men who aren't drunks, gamblers, or in debt"—she stopped to take a deep breath—"are probably rare in small towns. Big cities, too. I can testify to that."

"Mom, I like Wes, but if we do get together, I doubt it will last long. I'm not ready for a relationship with anyone but Finn. I hope you won't make a big thing out of it."

"I won't do that, honey. You've been through a horrific year, and I just want you to have fun and enjoy yourself. Nothing more."

"Really? Does Wes look like a fun guy to you?"

A small laugh escaped her mother's lips, and her face lit up with humor. "Of course not. But, darling, no one would ever call you a fun girl, either."

Hayley groaned. "So true. But what about Blake? He looks like a fun guy to me."

"He has a twinkle in his eyes," Susan said.

"When he was looking at you, he smoldered. I'm surprised smoke wasn't puffing out of his ears."

"I hope you're right. Single men my age aren't exactly filling up the streets in this place. Especially tall, lean, and handsome men. I can imagine him in an old Western, can't you?"

"I haven't watched a lot of old Westerns, but I suppose he'd be good in them."

"Not just good. *Yummy.*"

Hayley groaned again. "Too much information, Mom."

Susan laughed. "Blake makes furniture, then sells it. That's sexier to me than a man who rides horses. Plus, he'll be able to help us in our new business. If I could make a list of what I wanted out of a perfect man, he'd be in the top three."

Hayley wondered who the other two in the top three were but decided it was better not to know. "Mom, I love you."

"I love you, too. And this sweetie pie." Susan bent to kiss Finn's forehead. Straightening, she said, "I'm in love with the most handsome guy in the town, and he's sitting right in my lap."

"Me, too." Love for her mother and son welled up inside Hayley.

"We don't *need* men." Susan grinned. "They come in handy sometimes, especially with the procreation issue. And I have to admit that it's nice to have someone with muscles around to help with something mechanical. Other than that, I've lived a happy life without committing to any man."

"Right." Hayley nodded fiercely. Then she sat back, and she immediately thought about having sex with Wes. Would she be on top because of his leg? Or could they fit each other in sideways?

Because if they kept on seeing each other, it would probably happen. Not that it meant anything serious. She would be using him—*enjoying* him—and he would be enjoying her. Nothing else. Nothing more. Neither of them taking advantage of each other, just a win-win.

In the end, she was a lot like her mother. Maybe some people believed in love between a man and a woman. Maybe some people had found that love. But she had already found the love of her life. Right now, her mother was holding him, telling him how handsome and smart he was.

She loved both of them so much. If anything happened to them…

Her breath sucked in and her hands curled tight. This baby she hadn't wanted was her life. If need be, she would do anything to protect him. Do anything to keep him safe.

If need be, even murder. She doubted it would come to that, but if it did, she'd do whatever it took to protect him.

WES and his uncle sat on two stools by a table near the pub's front window. An old Tim McGraw country song was playing loud enough for them to hear the tune but not too loud that they couldn't hear each other talking. The place was about two-thirds full, more men than women, but the women were laughing more.

Glancing around, Wes realized that he knew everyone in the place. Knew about their wives and husbands and even ex-wives and ex-husbands. Knew if they had kids or grandkids. Knew if they drank too much or had a health problem or—in a few cases—were cheating on their spouses. People walked in and said hi to him and Blake and Spock, who lay at the side of Wes's chair. Spock gave them a doggy smile, and they all walked away grinning.

Nothing like having a dog to make friends quickly, though Wes gave equal credit to his uncle. If it hadn't been for Blake, he'd probably be in his kitchen every night, eating fast food or baking a frozen pizza in the oven.

"So," Blake said, "you and Hayley, huh?"

Wes narrowed his eyes, then took a gulp of his beer.

Blake grinned. "That's all right. You don't have to say anything. I could tell the minute you and she walked back in the house with Spock. I could practically see the sparks."

"You're imagining things. There's nothing to see or tell."

"Maybe not yet, but soon."

Wes set his beer bottle carefully on the table. "I don't like talking about this. I'm not asking anything about you and Susan."

"Whoa." Blake held up his left hand. "I don't talk about it, either. Just mentioning it because, hey ... it was hard to miss. Besides, hooking up with someone is a step forward in life. A step of healing. You aren't having those kind of thoughts if you're dying or in pain or if you mentally opted out of life."

"Yeah, well, all I'll say is that I'm not opting out of life. Physically or mentally."

Grinning, Blake leaned forward and slapped him on his arm. "That's what I was talking about."

Lucy came over to take their order. Her stomach was rounded now, about the size of a beach ball. "You two are glowing. Something good happening in your lives? Sold some furniture?"

They looked at each other. Blake smirked, and Wes held back a laugh, feeling lighthearted for the first time since ... well, since he'd looked out the window of his bedroom and saw Hayley's breasts in her bedroom window. He lifted his beer to his lips, letting his uncle reply.

"I think we're about to make a big sale," Blake said, "and soon."

Wes choked on the beer. Lucy slapped his back, Blake guffawed, and Spock barked.

Bending forward, Wes coughed up the beer that had gone down the wrong way. He and his uncle were acting like two teenage boys instead of men. *Welcome to the land of the living,* he thought. It was juvenile, uncomfortable, and probably not always good for him.

All because of a woman.

She was probably thinking the same thing about him.

He grabbed a napkin and hoped she was thinking of him and was having trouble waiting, because he sure the hell was.

If she felt the same way, and they did get together, how would they do it?

He took a slug of his beer. This would be the first time with a woman since he'd gotten out of the hospital.

Would he keep his prosthetic leg off or leave it on?

Would he be any good on top?

Would they be side by side?

Or would she be on top?

"What are you thinking?" his uncle asked.

"I'm thinking ... a lot of things."

"I bet."

"Not just about Hayley."

"Of course not. A man can't think about a woman all the time."

Wes took another sip of beer. Enough about his future sex life that he might or might not have. He needed a change of subject. "I heard that the guy who lives in the big house behind us—the former bed-and-breakfast—is back in town with his songwriter wife."

"Chuck," Blake said. "That's his name. I dated his mother once."

"How'd that work out?"

"I liked her fine. I think the feeling was mutual. But she was too uptight for me, and I was too loose for her."

"Why is it you always think women you dated liked you?"

"Women always like me. I'm just a likable guy. Besides, about ten years ago, I sanded and refinished a bureau and a chest of drawers for her. I gave her my friend discount. Why would it bother you?"

"It doesn't. I'm just glad there's no bad feelings. His son is setting up his Art Mart on the outskirts of town, with pole buildings for the artists, and he's adding a few buildings for craftsmen."

His uncle sat straighter in his chair and nodded for him to go on.

"I was thinking," Wes continued, "that you might ask him if we could showcase your furniture and my lights in one of the buildings."

"That's a great idea. We could ask a few other craftspeople to join us."

"Like Susan?"

Blake didn't agree, but he didn't disagree, either.

Wes knew what that meant. "You're sure it's a good idea? Mixing business and pleasure?"

"Whatever happens between Susan and me, I'm guessing we'll still be friends. She's that kind of woman."

"And you're that kind of man," Wes said.

His uncle chuckled. "No matter what happens between us, we could work together without discomfort."

"If you're sure," Wes said slowly, "it's all right with me if you ask her."

Blake leaned forward, his elbows on the table. "You don't sound convinced, but even without her furniture painting, Susan would be an asset. Men and women, no matter if they're young or old, like being around her. She has a personality that draws in people of any sex and age. Just to be around her, people feel happy. And when they feel happy, they'll spend money."

"I've never heard you talk about anyone like that."

Blake shrugged, sitting back.

"Okay," Wes said. "You convinced me. You should ask her to join us. We'd be idiots if we didn't."

"It wouldn't be my first idiot move—or my hundredth. Maybe I'm getting smarter with age. And her daughter. You'd like Hayley to be a part of it, wouldn't you?"

Now it was Wes's turn to shrug. "It's up to her, not me."

His uncle laughed out loud. Wes grinned and grabbed a handful of chips.

One thing about women, they made life more interesting. At least that's what his next-door neighbor did for him. Hayley gave him a reason to look out his bedroom window every morning … just in case she was standing in front of her window with her top off again—this time on purpose, waiting for him to see her.

That wasn't likely to happen again, and he was probably a pervert for thinking about it way too much, but a guy could hope.

18

YURI SAT ON THE BURGUNDY LEATHER CHAIR ACROSS from Leo's mother, who sat stiffly behind her desk. The home office had carved wood around the doorways and a ceiling that reminded him of a picture he'd seen of a room in a Russian palace. He leaned back and relaxed as well as he could against the high-backed chair. If Olga thought this room would intimidate him, she had chosen the wrong man.

He assessed her under his half-lidded eyes. He knew her from weddings and funerals and the kind of events that he couldn't avoid without offending a few relatives. He preferred not to be on close terms with her husband. Yuri had never liked being part of a pack. Especially a pack that reminded him of hungry wolves.

At first glance, Olga was a typical mob wife. Her skin was stretched tight, not a wrinkle in sight, but at least she wasn't starving herself, like some of the other wives. Her formerly brown hair was now blond. The last time Yuri had seen her husband, a curvy woman in her twenties had been hanging on Peter's arm. That wasn't anything unusual.

But right now, Olga was sitting straight, her lips pressed into a line as waves of intense emotion vibrated off of her.

This was the true Olga. He would bet money that she was far from a typical mob wife. He would bet more money that she wasn't a typical anything.

"Yuri, it's been a while," Olga said. "How is your mother?"

"She's doing well."

"I heard she moved to Ohio." Olga shuddered. "So cold there."

He nodded. Knowing his mother, she and her husband of two years were keeping each other warm in ways he didn't want to think of. "She says that she enjoys the snow."

"Perhaps I'm wrong about Ohio," Olga said. "After all, our families came from a much colder place. What does your father say about your mother's remarriage?"

"He says he's happy if she's happy."

"He must have mellowed."

Yuri shrugged. His father had been a drunk and then an addict before he'd landed in prison. Without prison, he'd probably be dead now.

Yuri's mom had divorced him more than a year before she'd met and then married a bus mechanic who'd decided to go back to his home in Ohio and buy a bus company in a small county. Not a glamorous occupation, but it was steady, legal, and it wouldn't land him in prison.

Most important, his mother loved him.

"You didn't call me here to talk about my parents," he said.

"You want to get right down to it?"

He raised his eyebrows, not replying.

She leaned slightly toward him. "I've heard you can do what no one else can do."

"Not true." He wanted to laugh but kept a straight face. This morning he was with the wife of a Mafia boss. Tonight he was meeting a US Marshal. Not his usual day. "I'm just a man. I can't create miracles."

"You can kill, can't you? And make it seem like someone else did it?"

"I could but I won't. I'm not an assassin. I don't kill."

"If you were offered enough money, you would do it."

"Why me? Why not take this to Peter?"

"You *know* why I'm asking you. Is sex more important to you than money?"

The nerves of his body tightened, sending out danger signals, but he forced himself to remain relaxed. So Olga knew he and Polina had made love last night. Or, if she wasn't certain, she suspected.

Was Polina's cell phone hacked? Her house bugged? Or was someone stalking her? Spying on her?

"I've never needed to choose one over the other," he said, keeping emotion out of his voice.

"Perhaps my wording wasn't clear. I should say that having sex with my son's bride is the choice you seem to find important now. The woman who is the reason my son is in prison."

He forced himself to relax. To not show any reaction. "That doesn't sound like the Leo I know. I wasn't aware that he would let himself be led by a woman."

"He's a man." Her hands on the desktop curled into fists. "She *knew* about his plans. She didn't speak to *me* about it. She told him it was a terrible idea, but she didn't stop him."

The air thickened with her anger. He waited a moment before he spoke with purposeful lack of emotion. "You must have mistaken me for a psychiatrist as well as a murderer. I'm neither."

"What *are* you? What exactly do you do?"

"Many things. What do you want from me?"

She leaned forward. "My grandson."

"I don't know where he is or where he would be."

"Don't lie to me. I know you're seeing my daughter-in-law. I know that if she contacted you, it's only for one reason."

He kept his gaze on her face but he didn't reply. Most people thought that the person who spoke the loudest won. They were wrong. In his experience, the person who *listened* the hardest ended up the winner.

"My son is in prison," she said finally, her voice clear. "I can't change that. He's not a perfect man. I know that he's led by his libido, and his ego is bigger than his brain. His father knows that, too. He's our son, and we can't change him. But what I *can* do is find our grandson and take charge of him."

He continued to look at her, still not replying.

A moment passed before she spoke again. "*This time* we'll do better. *This time,* we'll raise him right."

"You know that it's a boy?"

"The woman birthed a healthy boy. We were told that and nothing more. We told Leo, of course, and he told Polina."

He nodded, wondering how much money they'd paid for that small amount of information. He guessed they had paid off someone in the hospital.

"Peter and I want to raise the boy," she continued. "We won't make the same mistakes we did with Leo. The boy will grow up to be a better man than his father. A stronger man. A man not so easily led."

There was a stillness inside of Yuri. "You want a second chance. A do-over."

She shrugged. "Call it what you will. I know my daughter-in-law wants the baby boy, too. If she did sleep with you, that's the only reason. She'll do anything to find the child. Without the child, she will be nothing in this family. And don't bother to deny it, because I won't believe you."

He purposely let seconds tick by, watching her jaw and her shoulders stiffen before he replied. "You may know your daughter-in-law, but you don't know me. She may or may not want something, but I don't jump to her tune any more than I jump to yours."

As she processed his words, her eyes didn't leave his face. He felt as if she were trying to peer through his skin and skull bones to read the thoughts whirling through his brain.

"I bet you play a good game of chess," he said.

"I have no doubt that I would have, but my father only played chess with my brothers."

"Ah."

"Don't analyze me." Her tone sharpened. "We've talked in circles enough. You know what I want. It's time to make a deal."

"You're miles ahead of me. You may have plans, and your daughter-in-law may have plans, but the truth is that I have no plans."

She flattened her hands on the desktop. "I realize that you think I'm cold. After all, I have two daughters, and they have children."

"And their children are daughters, too."

Her face tightened more, her nostrils flaring.

"It's my opinion," he continued, "that women can be just as cruel and immoral as men."

She stared at him for a long moment, then her face moved. He thought it might be humor, but he wasn't sure until she laughed, a rusty *caw-caw-caw* sound.

He relaxed. She wasn't going to order anyone to kill him. At least, not at this moment.

"I can see why my daughter-in-law is attracted to you." Though her laughter had stopped, her face was more relaxed. "You are unusual among the men we know. You actually like women, don't you?"

He bowed his head slightly.

"How did your mother do this? I know it wasn't your father. He was always one of us. What did she know that the other wives didn't know?"

He shook his head. He could have told her what his mother had known. Joy. Laughter. She'd taught him how to dance, not how to hate. Taught him to enjoy life.

His father had loved her, but in his own way. Like a dog he loved and fed and protected—until he became a drunk and then an addict who could only think of himself. His mother's life was good now. She was happy, and he was happy for her.

"Never mind." Olga waved her fingers in the air, as if she were brushing away a fly. "Peter wants Leo's son as much as I do."

"That's not my problem."

"Of course not. What it could be is your solution."

"Solution to what?"

She leaned forward, her elbows on the table, her brown eyes glittering. "To anything you ever wanted."

A shiver went through him, tiny fingers of temptation dancing on his skin. It wasn't the first time. Though he thought of himself as his own man, he sure as hell wasn't an angel. He could be bought.

But only if it suited him.

"Let's get down to business." Her eyes shone brighter. She sensed that she had his attention now. "My daughter-in-law is paying you to find the baby, right?"

He straightened, not replying.

"Come." She snapped her fingers imperiously. "Tell me the truth. I know this already, and it won't be a betrayal. Are her skills in the bedroom worth a million dollars? You know she won't stay with you. You know she'll leave you for another man. That's the kind of woman she is."

Something inside him repudiated her words, but he didn't reply.

"I know Polina is paying you to find the baby." Her brown eyes darkened, and her tone lowered. "She wants him. And I want him."

"I'll tell you the same thing I told your daughter-in-law." He stood and looked down at her. "I don't know where the child is."

"But you can find out." She stood, too. "You're known for your ingenuity. You're known for doing the impossible."

"I'm not God."

"Of course not. You're much closer to the devil."

"I imagine you're on familiar terms with Satan, too."

"Are you taking this personally? You shouldn't. That's a waste of time and emotion."

He bowed his head slightly. She was correct. He and she were more alike than he was comfortable with.

"I'm glad we understand each other," she continued. "Frankly, I have plans for Polina that I will put into place as soon as... Well, never mind. When the time comes, she'll be taken care of. Until then, she can fuck you if she wants."

He stood still without replying.

"If you value your life," she said, "you won't repeat a word I've said."

"I don't repeat conversations."

"That's something else I heard about you." She leaned forward slightly. "I can be very generous when I get what I want. And I want the baby badly."

He just looked at her, not saying anything, resisting temptation, though it would be easier to ask, *How much?*

But if he asked that question, he might be tempted to agree.

Her lips curled up slightly, as if she were reading his mind. "A million dollars. That's how much I'll give you. That's how much my grandson will be worth."

He let a moment pass as his body felt cold and then hot. And then sick.

"You're asking for the impossible," he said, stepping back. "Don't waste your breath bargaining with me. Not on this. There are reasons I'm an independent. There are things that I won't do. Trafficking with women. Trafficking with drugs. And trafficking with babies. I don't touch any of those. Not with anything."

Silence crackled in the office. He turned—

"Ten million," she said.

He stopped and thought of all he could do with ten million. Tax free, too.

He didn't answer, but he quickened his strides, walked swiftly out of her office as if the devil were chasing after him.

Two women wanted the same thing from him. He could take Door Number One: make one happy and the other unhappy.

Or there was Door Number Two. He'd be a wealthy man. Wasn't that what every man wanted?

Or he could tell both of them he would do what they wanted. He could take their money and run. It was possible he could fool both of them.

Of course, his mother might be killed. Olga might send someone to Ohio to shoot her. She might even have his father in prison killed.

Or he could decide which woman he wanted to please.

Then there was Door Number Three. He could walk away from both women.

Or he could make his own Door Number Four. He just had to figure out what that door was and where it would lead. Because if he wasn't careful, it might lead straight to his grave.

19

THE DOORBELL WOKE HAYLEY. AS SHE FORCED OPEN HER eyelids that seemed to be stuck together, Finn cried, a howl that said he wanted his diaper changed and he wanted to eat. And he wanted it all *right now*.

When he stopped to suck in air before he let go of another hungry cry, she heard a pitter-patter of rain. She threw off the blanket and shivered. It wasn't just rain, either. It was a cold rain.

The doorbell rang again.

She had to pee.

She had to change Finn's diapers.

She had to feed him.

And she had to see who was at the door, because her mother wasn't answering it.

She grabbed Finn from his bassinet and tugged him to her right shoulder over her flannel pajamas, which she was glad she'd bought last week. Even in the coldest months, Miami was warmer than May in Door County. All this town needed was Eskimos and whales, and Hayley was sure that any Alaskan would feel right at home.

The doorbell rang again.

Finn drooled on her flannel-covered shoulder as she hurried to the door, the up-and-down half run momentarily stopping his loud cries. It also kick-started her brain as she remembered her mother had said she was leaving early this morning to go to Gills Rock, a small town at the end of the Door Peninsula, to check out chairs that someone was selling cheap. Susan had seen the pictures online last night and wanted to snap up the chairs before someone else did.

Hayley reached the front door. Looking out the small spy hole, she saw Wes and his dog. She opened the door, stepped back, then shoved Finn at him. "Hold the baby," she said, then turned and ran to the bathroom.

Behind her, Finn bellowed, and she ran faster. She didn't need to read her daily horoscope to realize that this was not an auspicious beginning of her day.

WES STOOD in the hallway jiggling the baby to stop his cries. Next to him, Spock had his head up, sniffing the baby's butt, clearly captivated by the scent. Hayley returned in a couple of minutes, taking fast steps toward them, her hair uncombed and messy, no makeup on her face, and wearing soft-looking flannel pajamas.

She was a mess. And the sexiest woman he'd seen in ... maybe ever, though he admitted there had been a long dry stretch before he'd met her.

Finn hollered, obviously wanting his mommy and tired of Wes's jiggling. Hayley held out her arms, and Wes handed the baby over to her.

"Thanks," she said.

Finn wailed again, and Wes winced for her. "I can change the diaper while you change your clothes," he said, following her down the hallway.

"Who said I'm going to change?" She turned into her bedroom.

"Uh ... not me. You like coffee? I can make some."

"Black works for me. I'll be ready in a few minutes."

He made his coffee, and then he went into the living room. There were two more chairs, which made the room crowded. These two were a burnt orange, smaller than the other recliners. He liked the color. It stood out without being too red or too orange or too brown.

He sat in one, and it was comfortable. He pulled a wooden lever on the right, and the footrest whipped up. It could be a little longer, but still very nice. Closing his eyes, he allowed himself to relax.

A satisfied sigh came from his left side. He opened his eyes and glanced down at Spock, who was making himself comfortable on the carpet next to him.

It felt good to be here in this home. His place felt temporary. This place, with a baby and his mom—and the four recliners—felt like a home.

He closed his eyes again...

SPOCK RAISED HIS HEAD, looking up at Hayley. She put her index finger over her mouth. Spock seemed to know it meant *quiet*, because he rested his head on the carpet next to Wes's recliner again. She turned her attention back to Wes. With his eyes shut, he looked younger. At peace. Too peaceful to waken.

She tiptoed to the bathroom for a quick shower. Finn was in the small playpen in her bedroom. His diaper had been changed, and he'd been fed. He should be fine for a short time.

She didn't like to leave him alone too long, though her mother said she worried too much. Susan didn't understand that she wasn't worrying. She wasn't preparing for the worst. She was just making sure that everything was done right. It made her feel as if she had some kind of control when, for nine months, her control had been stolen from her.

She whipped through her shower, dried off, then hurried to her bedroom and changed into jeans and a sweatshirt. In the playpen, Finn looked up and chortled. His arms splayed out, he rocked from side-to-side, laughing. A baby boy in a blue jumper, with orange curls on his head, fed and clean and happy.

"I'll be right back," she said.

He chortled again, shaking the rattle.

"Hey," Wes said behind her, his voice husky.

She snapped around. He and Spock stood in the doorway. He smiled at her, and she felt warm inside. No, not warm. Melty. Like cheddar cheese on crusty bread on a hot grill.

"Need me to do anything?" he asked.

"Well, it's been five days since our discussion." The words blurted out of her—and she wasn't sorry. She looked him in the eyes, her chin up.

She trusted this man. He was a man she could count on.

"You mean it?" he asked, his eyes burning.

"Finn's awake now. I'll have to wait until he's asleep. Tonight?"

"Tonight. Yes."

Finn was gurgling, his own happy sounds. Spock breathed heavily. She gazed down and saw that his mouth was open, and he looked happy, too.

"The baby and the dog are approving," she said.

"I knew my dog was smart."

"And my son."

They grinned at each other.

"Is that why you came?" she asked.

"I almost forgot." The corners of his eyes crinkled. "Once you brought up sex, everything else flew out of my mind."

She laughed, and her face warmed.

"Chuck," he said, "the neighbor who lives in the big house behind my place, has set up an Art Mart for the tourist season."

"I heard about it. In the big pole building, right? At the end of town?"

"That's it. It's a place for local artists to sell their work. Chuck's setting up another pole building for designers who specialize in furniture and lighting. House stuff. Uncle Blake and I and a couple of other designers are showcasing a few items. We have space for a couple of your mom's recliners. Or something else if she prefers. It just can't be too big."

"Will we have to pay for a slot?"

"Yes. Is that a problem?"

"I'll ask my mother, but I think she'll do it. She's almost always ready for something new. I'm more..." She sighed. "I *used* to be more conservative. Now, I'm not conservative at all."

"You're a risk taker now?" He grinned.

"You're making fun of me, but you should've seen me before."

"What I see right now looks pretty good to me."

Her cheeks warmed, and she knew they were turning pink. "So, you want me to tell my mom? Is that why you came over?"

"No. I want to offer you a job. We're setting up a website. Your mom mentioned to my uncle that you're good with computers."

"I could do that. So, that's why you came over?"

"Uh huh. And the sex, of course."

She laughed, feeling happy inside in a way that had been a long time coming.

"If the baby falls asleep early," he said, "call me. You have my phone number."

"I'll throw pebbles at your window."

He laughed, a lusty sound. She watched the man and the dog step outside, then the door closed behind them.

She turned to Finn. "Guess whose mommy is going to get lucky tonight?"

Finn flapped his hands, like a dolphin flapping its tail, and made a string of happy sounds. She laughed, feeling dolphin-happy herself. This evening, she hoped to be even happier.

She told herself not to expect too much, but she still couldn't stop the happiness leaking out of her pores.

Then she realized the leakage wasn't happiness. It was milk from her breasts. She looked down at the damp spots on her gray top, and she groaned. Then her groans switched to laughter, and she slid down onto the floor, holding on to her stomach while Finn made happy noises along with her.

"I love you," she said.

He smiled at her and said, "Gah."

"Mommy hopes she'll be happy today."

"Gah!"

"Happier than normal, but you know I'm always happy when I'm with you."

"Gah!" he said.

"Gah!" she said, and he laughed.

She pushed herself up from the floor. "I'll be back. I need to wash up."

As she strode to the bathroom, she thought that she and her neighbor might make a pair today. Her with her leaky breasts and him with part of his leg missing.

Not very romantic, but that was okay. Neither of them had pretended to be perfect. The only thing they wanted was to make love. Not that she expected—or wanted—*love*. Right at this time in her life, she just wanted to get laid. To get tuned up.

She could think of cruder terms, but that's what she craved right now. Sex was a biological need, and love and marriage—even a happily-ever-after love—were not necessary or required. Though she'd been more discerning in her sexual partners than many of her friends—until her last horrible lapse of judgment—she had normal needs.

At least she knew Wes, and she trusted him. She admired his character and his person.

Besides, he was a dog lover. And he'd changed Finn's diaper.

If that didn't put him in the nice-guy category, she didn't know what would.

20

IT WAS EVENING IN MIAMI. SOMEONE IN YURI'S neighborhood was playing music loudly. The sound seeped into his house, fast and sexy and Cuban, as Polina lay on the bed, her body satisfied, feeling the heat from her recent coupling with Yuri.

After their first time, she hadn't planned on coming back—she had just thought it would be a one-time thing—but Yuri's lovemaking was sweet. Sweeter than her favorite Swiss chocolate. Sweeter than gooey marshmallows. Sweeter than her favorite ... well, pretty much anything.

She sighed. Of course, this sense of satisfaction wasn't going to last. It was just temporary. Yuri was just so good at this, taking his time and finding all the spots that made her crazy. Making love to Yuri was like falling into a pool of warm honey, a pool she wanted to remain in for a long and very slow time.

So different from Leo's fast-and-furious method of lovemaking, which meant he was usually done before her.

"What are you thinking?" Yuri asked. His mellow baritone sent a small shiver through her. He slid his arm under her shoulder, tugging her close to him.

She sighed in contentment. "I'm thinking that you're a master of sex."

He laughed. "What a coincidence. I see you as the mistress of sex."

She rolled onto her side to face him. There was a sheet over their bodies. Not because of modesty but because there was a small chill in the air. "I like sex, but I'm not into whips or hurting or being hurt. Just bawdy, wonderful, sweaty sex."

He smiled, his arm still around her. Not like a man claiming his woman—as if she were his property—but just a normal man-and-woman thing.

Affection. That's what it was. He felt affection for her.

She shivered.

"Cold?" he asked.

"No, just a thought. I should leave now."

He frowned. "Are you worried someone might find out you're cheating on Leo and will tell him?"

"Do *you* worry about it?"

"Should I worry?"

"I've never cheated on him before you. And the woman who had his baby was not the first."

"Yes, but he's the boss man's son," Yuri said.

She sat up, letting the sheet slide down to her thighs. "The baby is a boy. That much was leaked. You don't know how much that means to Leo's father. Male babies are everything to him and to Leo."

"So if you possess the baby, he'll be your leverage?"

"I won't be just Leo's wife. Marriage means nothing to Leo or his father. What matters is that I'll be the mother of the baby who might someday be in Peter's position, whether I birthed him or not."

"They still won't like it if they know you're sleeping with me."

"Once I find the baby and take him home, no one will care whether I'm sleeping with you or anyone else. Only the baby will matter. As the baby's mother, I'll matter, too. No one will be able to deny me. Not even if Leo rots in jail."

There was a moment of silence.

"You hate him, don't you?" Yuri asked.

"No." She shook her head, because she was realizing something. Realizing a terrible, terrible thing. "It's not him that I hate," she said in a hushed voice.

"What is it?" He turned onto his side.

The room was dark, but the shade was up, and the light from the half-moon in the sky angled into the bedroom. It was just light enough to see his soft lips and the spark in his eyes.

She could almost feel that there was more than sex tonight. That he cared for her. That she cared for him.

"I don't know." She lay back down, turned to him, and put her arms around his shoulders. "I don't know anything for sure. And I don't really want the baby because he would be part of the brotherhood. That's *not* the reason I'm doing it."

"What is the reason?"

"Truthfully? Maybe Leo is right. Maybe I won't ever get pregnant. Maybe this might be my last chance to have a baby. After all, Leo *is* the baby's father, and he's still my husband." She paused for a moment before asking in a low voice, "Am I horrible for wanting this?"

He pressed his warm lips against her forehead then kissed her lips softly. "You're not horrible. I don't know all the answers. I only know one thing."

She was afraid to ask. Afraid to hear insincere flattery. Or he might say they had to stop this. It was too dangerous, and they couldn't do this again.

"I know that you feel good in my arms," he said, his voice husky.

She sighed. She would leave. Soon. Very soon.

Instead, she closed her eyes and just breathed. Breathing was good. Thinking was overrated.

His body relaxed, and so did hers. Maybe she could sleep a little. What would it hurt?

But as he slept, she thought of the mother who was breaking the marshal's code to save her child.

A great sacrifice.

She thought of the mother who was letting her son give a kidney to the child so he could go to college.

Another sacrifice.

She thought of the woman Leo had tricked into pregnancy. The woman could have hated the baby because of what Leo had done. She could have denied it. She could have made a deal with Olga and Peter. Or with her. Given her the baby. After all, Leo had betrayed her.

Instead, she'd taken the baby with her to an unknown place. A sacrifice.

And the woman's mother, another Miami native, had left with her. Another sacrifice.

Polina turned her head away from Yuri, and she cried softly until she finally fell asleep, tears staining her face, knowing the sacrifice she needed to make.

"FINN'S ASLEEP," Hayley said on her cell phone.

"I'll be there in a few minutes," Wes said.

Hayley picked up a book and sat down on a recliner to read while she waited. She'd only read four pages when a knock sounded on the front door. She set down the book and pushed off of the recliner. As she hurried to the front door, her heart thumped.

Though she knew it must be Wes, she still turned on the outside light and peeked out the spyhole. It was him, of course. She opened the door and stepped back to let him in. It was chilly out, and he wore a blue long-sleeved top and jeans.

Spock stood at Wes's side, his tail wagging, his mouth open in a big smile. He looked good with a doggy smile.

Wes looked even better. He gazed at her, as if drinking her in with his eyes, while Spock's tail wagged wildly, as if she were the one person he'd been waiting for in his entire doggy life.

She greeted Wes, then bent down to pet Spock, putting her arm around his neck, and getting a damp tongue wash on her right cheek as Wes closed the front door behind him.

"You know my mom's not here?" she asked, standing again.

"Uncle Blake told me not to call him or stop by his place tonight. He said he had company. I was pretty sure he meant your mother."

"Um, do you want anything to drink?" she asked, then grimaced. "I'm so bad at this. I'm not used to seducing men."

"I'd guess that men usually seduce you."

"Not that many. And it's been a long time. More than a year."

"Longer for me."

"You want something to drink?" she asked, and her voice wobbled.

"Do you?" He took a step toward her.

"No. I told you I'm not good at seduction."

"That makes two of us. But I'm willing to try."

"Me, too." She swallowed, feeling awkward. She'd never been the instigator. Of course, she'd never been with a man like Wes before. A man who had an inner strength in him. A man who had a hurt in him, too.

She suspected he had a mild version of PTSD—post-traumatic stress disorder. Not a version that kept him from living his life, but a version that left a sadness inside of him.

The thought made it easier to step forward, her arms out. As she took another step, his arms rose up to her, too, and he drew her to him.

She leaned against him and sighed. Her breasts pressed against his chest; her lower body found the place to nestle into between his slightly spread legs.

He sighed, too. A sigh that said, *I'm home now.*

That was exactly how she felt. As if, after years of searching, she'd come home.

Her head tilted up, and then they were kissing, mouths open, tongues exploring, arms tightening. She stood on her tiptoes, and their pelvises bumped nicely.

A small noise came from her throat.

He moved and started to fall to the left. His hands tightened on her back, gripping her for support.

She held him as he swore. "I've got you," she whispered. "I'm not letting you go."

"I'm making a mess of this," he said.

She curved her right hand on the side of his face and stared into his brown eyes. She saw the frustration in his face. Felt his anger at himself.

She understood. She knew that frustration. Knew that anger.

Pushing up on her tiptoes again, she kissed his lips softly. Not intensely like before. This was an *it's going to be okay* kiss.

"We're not doing this standing up. Let's go into the bedroom." She gripped his hand and turned, then drew him behind her, taking her time because she knew men hated to show their weaknesses. As if women didn't have weaknesses and vulnerabilities and chinks in their nonexistent armor.

He followed her. As they reached her bedroom, she paused and whispered, "The bassinet's in here with Finn in it. We're going to my mother's room. I'll change the sheets in the morning." She grimaced. "It's the first time I haven't slept in the same room with him since he left the hospital. I was always afraid someone would try to steal him."

"Would you like Spock to guard him?"

"You would do that?"

He smiled slowly. "I don't think I'll need Spock for the rest of the night."

She choked back a laugh, then watched as Wes walked with Spock into the room. Saying something in a low voice to Spock, he made a hand signal. Spock lay down next to the bassinet.

Tears warmed her eyes, and she wiped them away as he came out of the bedroom, leaving the door open.

She sniffed and led the way to her mother's room. It was crazy that they had to do things like this, but she'd never felt so cared for by a man who wasn't her father. Never felt so valued.

They reached her mother's bedroom, and she gestured at the queen-sized bed. "Here it is." She turned to him. "The time and the place."

"And the man and the woman," he said. "I've been practicing push-ups."

"For me?" She laughed, and heard the breathlessness of her voice.

It was going to be all right, after all.

They kissed, and she felt a melting inside her, a softness and a strength, even as the center of her heated up. They were still fully clothed. He still wore a jacket, though it was unzipped—and except for the one kiss and the body-to-body hug, they had done nothing sexual.

But lately just looking into his eyes made her feel sensual. Made her feel warm. Made her feel that she wanted more.

"You can practice your push-ups another time." She stepped back. "For this time, I prefer to be the girl on top."

"I don't—"

She pulled off her top, and his words stopped as he stared at her breasts, his lips parted.

She wasn't wearing a bra.

"Enjoy the view while you can," she said. "Once I'm done with breastfeeding, they won't be this full."

"I'll never stop enjoying the view."

She laughed and shook her head. *Men*. They always lied when they wanted sex. Even when they already knew they were going to get lucky.

And tonight he would. Tonight they would *both* get lucky.

She draped the top over a trunk in the corner. Then she stripped off her pants and tossed them on the trunk.

He stared at her. Drinking in the sight of her.

She smiled. "Well? Are you keeping your clothes on?"

"I'll need to sit for part of this." He walked to the bed and sat down.

"Take all the time you want."

He took off his shirt first, then his jeans. His erection sprang up, and then she saw his below-the-knee prosthetic leg—a sleeve-like shape wrapped around his knee with a metal rod below.

"It looks like a work of art," she said.

"I've had that same thought. The best work of art that I'll ever have."

She put her hand on the sleeve around his knee. "It looks simple, but I know there's a lot more below this."

His stillness brought her gaze to his face.

"I looked it up," she said. "I wanted to know how they worked."

"I'm not surprised."

She smiled. "And I see something very impressive above your legs, too."

He laughed and held out his hands. "I'm ready now."

"I can see that. Are you leaving the prosthesis on?"

"That's a good question. Let's try it with the leg on the first time."

"The first time? You're counting on a second time?" She laughed, feeling a lightness inside her along with the heat, as if she was about to fly high up into the sky…

21

THE SOUND OF THE FRONT DOOR OPENING THE NEXT morning stirred Hayley out of a deep sleep. Half-awake and feeling satisfied—the way she hadn't felt for a long time—she rolled onto her back and stretched. Squeaky sounds came from the bassinet. She turned her head, the morning light peeking in through the blind slats. Her body felt fluid, as if she were made out of warm water, and she remembered last night.

Wes below her. Then Wes rolling above her.

Using his push-up skills after all.

The bedroom light on so they could see each other.

His face tense.

His eyes on hers.

Another squeak came from Finn. She blinked away the images, rolled out of bed, then leaned over the bassinet. The baby's eyes were closed. Good. Finn had woken up when Wes and Spock had left about five in the morning—longer than they'd planned, but they had fallen asleep. She'd fed Finn, then changed the sheets on her mother's bed. They were the same pale green color as the other ones, and she was sure her mom wouldn't notice.

At last, she'd gone to her room, put Finn into the bassinet again, and had fallen asleep again.

She looked at the clock on the dresser now. Ten after nine. Her mother said she'd be back by nine. Hayley knew she should step out into the hall to greet her mother. But she felt so loose and lovely and satisfied. She didn't want to lose this feeling yet.

Already, she wanted to do it again. Have sex with Wes. Soon. Very soon.

The baby made more noises. Louder noises. Any second now, the noises could turn into cries or even screams.

Her mom stuck her head into the bedroom. "Hey."

"Hey, Mom." Hayley picked up Finn. His eyes were wide open now. "Hi, sweetie. How's Mama's baby?"

He laughed and said a few incomprehensible syllables, his arms waving, happy now that he was getting some love from his mommy.

She kissed his warm cheek, and he laughed again. She carried him to the changing table. Susan dropped her purse, handed her a new diaper, then held out the bucket for the wet one.

"How was your night?" her mom asked.

"No complaints." Hayley quickly turned back to Finn. She'd learned the hard way not to leave him alone for more than a couple seconds with nothing covering his penis. She hurriedly put a diaper on him, then picked him up, held him against her, and turned back to her mom.

"I suppose in this small town," she said, "there will be gossip about you and Blake."

"I'm happy to give them entertainment," her mother said. "It was actually a pretty tame evening."

"Oh, Mom, I'm sorry."

"I didn't mean *boring*." Her mother reached out for her grandson, taking him from Hayley and cradling him in her arms. She finally looked up, a pensive look on her face. "It was ... very nice."

"*Very* nice?"

"Yes." Her mother nodded decisively. "*Very* nice."

Hayley raised her eyebrows as her mother frowned, still holding Finn. Not saying anything.

"Mom? Are you okay?"

"I'm fine. Just fine. I just..." With a sigh, Susan shrugged. "Everything is so *easy* with Blake."

"What's wrong with easy?"

"It's *too* easy. I'm not sure how I feel about it."

"You think he has a hidden agenda?"

"Men always have an agenda. But the thing is, Blake and I are kind of alike." Susan's brow furrowed. "I think that's it. He's the male *me*."

"Do you mean—"

"This is upsetting. I can't talk about it." Susan thrust Finn at her.

Hayley took him, then stared as her mother backed out of the room.

"I need to take a bath and think about this. I'm not sure if this is good or could turn into a disaster." Susan hurried away.

A demanding cry brought Hayley's attention back to Finn. She didn't know what was going on, but life was getting very curious. She'd thought it was going to be dull and boring in Trouble Bay, despite the inauspicious town name. Instead, it was unexpected and not boring at all.

A word lit up in her mind. *Trouble*. That's what it was. Trouble in Trouble Bay.

"THE DEAL IS DONE," Yuri said, talking on his burner phone in a street outside the hospital. Polina gasped, then for long moments, no words came through.

"Thank you," she said finally, her voice choked.

"Don't you want to know how much?"

"Oh. Yes. How much?"

"She wouldn't take two fifty, so I upped it to two seventy-five. She came back with a three hundred thousand demand, so I agreed for you. She's giving her son two fifty and keeping fifty for herself."

"She loves her son. I'm glad."

"I think she does. She said that if it really helps the other child, she'll feel good about it."

"You talked to the marshal?"

"Oh, yes. I just came out of the hospital." He glanced behind him. He preferred not calling the marshal on the phone, even with a burner phone. She could be recording him, but he was pretty sure that hadn't happened. He knew a desperate woman when he saw one.

"The marshal's son—"

"He's not getting better. The marshal's not ready to give you the address until his half brother is tested and he's cleared as a donor."

"How long—"

"The doctors want to set this up as fast as they can."

"It's urgent?"

"Life or death."

There was another moment of silence. "Then I don't feel bad about it," she said.

"If it goes through, it would be worth it. Both mothers would agree."

"But not the baby's mother. Not the woman my husband impregnated."

He didn't reply, listening to the wail of an ambulance.

"We're just trying to make ourselves feel like we're not doing anything wrong," she said, her voice so low he had to strain to hear it, especially with the screaming ambulance coming closer. "Aren't we?"

He didn't answer. Didn't say that she was the one who'd wanted this done. Because he was part of it, too.

"I won't see you tonight," she said.

"That's probably a good idea. When I hear from the marshal, I'll call you."

She hung up, and he headed to the car. Things were getting too complicated. It was best this way. He was getting used to her, and it was good that she was staying away, though he already missed her.

22

SITTING AT THE KITCHEN TABLE AND TYPING ON BLAKE'S laptop was not the way Hayley was used to working. But her last job had been in an office, during a time when she wasn't living in a house with her baby and her mother, and it had ended over a year ago.

"You know that I can babysit," Susan said.

Hayley raised her gaze to her mother, who was getting a glass of water. "You've done enough for me already. Besides, you have your own work now."

Her mother set the glass on the counter and turned from the sink. "Sweetie, *you* are my most important work."

Hayley choked up a little. "Mom, I want to be as good a mother as you are."

"You already are."

"Like every woman I know, I'm doing the best I can." Hayley sat back in the chair. "I have a few days to set up the website for the three of you. I can do it between nap times, and even when Finn's playing with his toys."

"You're enjoying this, aren't you?" Susan wiggled her fingers. "This computer magic."

"I wish it could be done by magic. It's more like a puzzle, and you know how much I enjoyed putting together puzzles as a child."

"I enjoyed puzzles as a child," Susan said, "but beyond the basics, I don't understand computers. You take after your father."

"Thanks, I think. You know he's going bald?"

"Your father looks very distinguished with balding hair."

"He does look cute." Hayley grinned. "Even when the top of his head is shiny."

"You have my hair, so that shouldn't be a problem for you. But you have your dad's personality. Sensible, levelheaded, and steady. Always thinking over a move before you make it."

"Sensible? Thinking over my moves? If that were true, why are we here?"

"Honey, even the most sensible person can be fooled. Before you dated the jerk, you checked him out, right?" She pointed at the laptop. "On the computer."

"Of course."

"There you go. You were given insufficient and incorrect information. If the computer didn't know, how were you supposed to know?"

"Mom, I love you."

Susan smirked. "Mothers are always right."

"I wish! I'm still learning." Hayley glanced down at the laptop. Time to change the subject. "I'm adding the photos you took. You did an amazing job. They're perfect."

Susan beamed. "I know you're changing the subject, but I thought the photos were good, too. Thank you!"

"Now I need a few reviews from people who've made purchases."

"I can give a review!"

"You can't do that," Hayley said. "You work with Blake. You're *intimate* with him."

Her mother straightened. "Blake and I are lovers, but that doesn't mean I would lie."

Hayley sighed. "Blake really does great work, but you're his colleague now. I'll email him and see if he can get quotes from two or three people who've bought his furniture. I'll ask Wes the same thing about his light fixtures. And you sold that sofa to the woman who works at the gas station."

"Annie," her mother said. "I gave the sofa to her for half price. She's three months pregnant. Her two brothers put the sofa in the back of their pickup, then took it to her apartment in Sturgeon Bay. She's living there with her boyfriend. He just got a job as a truck driver, and they don't have a lot of money."

"If the baby is a girl, maybe they'll name it after you."

Susan laughed. "I'd love it, but I'll be happy with a good review. And I painted Martha's two chairs and a couch, remember? She's the woman on the next block with the two poodles. I'm sure she'll say something nice."

"Two or three snippets of praise will be plenty," Hayley said. "Or even just one glowing line. And I think you should raise your prices."

"Blake's the one who should raise his prices. He's an artist."

"Tell him! Though I think you're an artist, too."

"You're right, I *am* an artist. And I have told him. He's thinking about it."

"That's good, but I prefer action over thinking."

"Or fantasizing." Susan laughed. "Most men fantasize that they're action characters. At least Blake *listens* to me, which is something a lot of men don't do. They listen to me when I say fun things. Laughing things. Happy things." She whisked her hand in the air. "All of that is fine, because I like fun and laughter and happiness. But I have other thoughts, too."

"I know you do. I listen to you."

"You're my daughter." Susan walked over to the table. "And you're also a woman. Blake is not related, and he's a man. He may listen, but that doesn't mean he's going to do what I say. He has a stubborn streak."

Hayley opened her mouth to tell her that Blake's nephew took after him that way when she noticed her mother was frowning, her hands twisted together.

"Mom, are you okay?" Hayley reached out and clasped her mother's hands. "This whole last year you've been my rock. If something's wrong, let me be your rock."

Tears sparkled in Susan's eyes, and Hayley worried more. Her mother wasn't a crier. Something must be seriously wrong.

"Are you sick, Mom?"

"Lovesick maybe." Susan gave a valiant laugh and pulled her hands from Hayley's. "I think my rock is crumbling."

"Mom! Is it possible that *you* are pregnant?"

"No!"

"You're in your early fifties. I've heard of women having babies even after fifty."

"That's *not* the reason I'm a little teary."

"Then what is it?"

Susan sucked in air, then exhaled it in a whoosh. "I hate to say this, but Blake might be the perfect man for me."

"Are you saying..." Hayley realized she was half standing, holding on to the back of her chair, her mouth gaping.

"That I love him?" Susan asked. "Is that what you're asking? It's early and I don't know for sure. Maybe it's just the great sex."

Hayley plopped back down on the chair.

Her mother laughed shakily. "Don't worry. I'm fine. I'm going to Sturgeon Bay to shop for material. Is there anything you need?"

"Just a minute." Hayley grabbed a pen and paper to jot down the items she needed to make baby food.

"You are a great mom," Susan said.

"Ditto." Hayley stood, then handed her the scribbled list. "And I have a great kid, too."

"The best," Susan said. "We *both* have the best kids."

Hayley hugged her. "You'll be all right. Mom. We'll both be all right."

Susan nodded, then stepped back. Instead of leaving right away, she sighed. "I hate to tell you this, but I don't want you to get blindsided."

"Blindsided?" Hayley stiffened.

"It's not *horrible*."

"Don't keep me in suspense. Tell me."

"Well… I'm pretty sure that at least half the Trouble Bay natives know Wes stayed over at our place the other night."

Hayley held back a groan.

"I'm sorry, honey. Apparently a neighbor spotted him and his dog leaving our house in the early dawn and sneaking back to his place."

"*Sneaking*?" Hayley shook her head. Her mother was probably being kind by saying only half the natives knew about her and Wes. It was probably closer to eighty percent. No doubt they knew about Susan and Blake, too, but the difference was that neither Susan nor Blake cared.

Hayley cared. After what she'd gone through in Miami, she cared too much.

"You're upset," Susan said. "Maybe I shouldn't have said anything."

"No, no, you're right." Hayley raised her chin. "So, they know Wes and I are sleeping together. We're adults. We're both single. So what is we're lovers?"

"Excellent attitude." But Susan didn't smile. And she didn't leave.

"There's something else, right?" Hayley didn't want to know, but she might *need* to know. "What are you holding back? What were you going to tell me?"

"Well..." Susan grimaced. "I like Wes a lot. But though he *seems* adjusted to the loss of his lower leg, sometimes I see him brooding."

"I brood sometimes, too. We're alike that way."

"I wish him well, but you've been through a lot already."

"We've all been through a lot. Me and you." Hayley gestured toward Wes's house. "Wes and Blake. If we all get old enough, we all get troubles."

"You're right, honey. Life isn't a fairy tale." Susan patted Hayley's cheek, then stepped back. "I'm going to the workshop now, but I just want to say that if Wes hurts you in any way, I might have to hurt him more."

She snapped around and hurried out of the kitchen, leaving Hayley standing with her mouth gaped open.

POLINA SAT in a room that her mother-in-law had styled after a parlor in the St. Petersburg Winter Palace, not realizing or caring that the gold fixtures and white-and-blue painted walls looked out of place in the vibrant city that beat with waves of heat nearly year round. Not that Polina was surprised. After all, Olga's heart was probably encased in ice. And the expensive décor didn't make up for the way her husband flaunted his mistresses.

"Is the coffee too strong?" Olga asked.

"It's fine," Polina said, though the thick, hot brew made her teeth ache. After another sip, she set it on the table. Just in case it was poisoned. Though she was not Sleeping Beauty, her mother-in-law probably had an ancestor who had taught her how to inject poison into apples and coffee.

Her mother-in-law's lips curved up, as if she read Polina's thoughts, and they amused her.

"You have something you wanted to say to me?" Polina asked.

"You're getting straight to the point." Olga set down her cup. "Good. So will I. I understand that you're seeing Yuri Petrov."

"I'm paying him to help me find Leo's baby."

Olga leaned forward, and her eyes blazed. "What does he know? You *have* to tell me."

"Nothing." Polina lowered her voice, trying to sound casual. "To tell you the truth, Yuri didn't want to do this. The woman and the baby are in the witness protection program now, and he thinks trying to trace her is a waste of time."

"But he did say yes?"

She nodded, forcing herself not to glance away from Olga.

"I talked to him, too," Olga said.

Polina stiffened.

"I offered him money, but he walked away."

"How much did you offer him?" Polina asked.

"Does it matter? I'm sure it's much more than you offered."

Polina relaxed slightly. If Yuri had said yes to Olga, Polina wouldn't be talking to her now.

"What *is* he doing?" Olga's eyes flashed. "What's he up to?"

"He told me he can't find out anything," Polina said, looking straight into Olga's eyes. "He says I'm wasting his time, and there's nothing more he can do."

"Do you believe him?"

"He can be ... independent."

"My mother would have called him a rogue," Olga said.

Polina sputtered a laugh, not expecting that. "My mother would have said that he doesn't work well with other children."

Olga smiled. A real smile. Usually Olga stared at her as if she were a bug that she wanted to grind beneath her sturdiest shoe.

What was she up to?

"I'll call Yuri again," Olga said. "If I persist, he'll change his mind."

Polina raised her eyebrows, not saying anything. Sometimes silence had more impact than words.

Olga's mouth flattened. "I can see you don't believe me. You forget how much money I can offer him."

"He's done trying to find her. He won't do it."

"I don't give up as easily as you."

Polina shrugged. If she kept arguing, Olga would suspect she had her own agenda—though she probably already did. And if Olga kept digging, she might find out the truth.

"You realize your money might not last forever?" Olga asked. "The house is in Leo's name, isn't it? It's not wholly paid for. Peter and I are fully aware of Leo's finances. He had a lot of money, but he lived large. He spent too much. If you plan on selling, you'll have to talk to his lawyer."

"I know this." She'd only found out a few days ago, but she knew a few other things that Olga didn't know. And she had her own timeline on when to leave.

Her investments, separate from Leo's, wouldn't allow her to live in an extravagant style, but she didn't want to live in an extravagant style. She'd done that, and it hadn't nurtured her. It hadn't filled her. It hadn't made her happy.

The thoughts surprised her, but she admitted the truth to herself. The money and her position had made her greedy.

Greedy enough to save one child so she could steal another.

"Well?" Olga asked, her voice sharp.

"I dismissed the staff two weeks ago," Polina said, her breathing harsh. "I have my jewelry. I might sell some of the more expensive pieces. Or all of them. I can live in a smaller home or apartment."

"Very sensible. You're more than a pretty face."

"So are you," Polina said.

Olga smiled slightly. "You would have made a good mother."

Polina's throat squeezed and tears sprang up in her eyes. She hadn't expected that.

Olga leaned forward. "If you need anything, you should call me."

Polina nodded, afraid if she opened her mouth, she would start bawling. All because Olga was nice to her.

Was it an act? It had to be.

"Our life..." Olga shook her head, the corners of her lips turned down. "What we do and how we live ... it's not a good life."

"Why do you do it?" Polina whispered. "Why do you stay?"

Olga looked at her for a long moment, her lips parted and her face so frozen and so sad that Polina got it. In the years that she'd been married to Leo, her mother-in-law had treated her like a non-person, not because she disliked her but because she was keeping her own emotions locked down inside of her. If she released them, her unhappiness would spew out of her like lava erupting from a volcano.

Polina stood. Her imagination was working overtime, her thoughts taking her to odd places. "I should go. If you want to call Yuri and ask him to find the baby, that will be your decision."

Olga got to her feet more slowly. "What if he does find the baby? What if he calls you?"

"He said he was done with it, and I'm taking him at his word."

"Of course you are." Olga's face turned cold again, her mask back on. "Of course."

Polina shivered, then turned and hurried away, glad to leave this house, where unhappiness clung to the walls, the floors, the ceilings.

And, most of all, to the woman who lived in it.

23

WES SAT ON THE PIER BEHIND HIS UNCLE'S HOUSE, A fishing pole in his hand, his dog at one side, his uncle on the other. The sun was shining down at them, not too hot and not too cold. There was a sweet-smelling breeze in the air, a mixture of lake and sunlight. It was the third week in May. Tourists were returning, more every week, which made the townspeople happy because more tourists meant more money.

When Wes had first moved out here, he hadn't been looking forward to the tourist season, but this last week he'd sold five of his lighting creations, and he'd found out one new thing about himself. He could be bought.

Two of the sales had been to Chuck's wife, who was a Grammy-winning songwriter and lived in the former bed and breakfast behind his house. She'd told Wes he should raise his prices. He'd laughed, but when he'd told Hayley, she'd opened her laptop and added an extra fifty dollars to his two smaller lamps and one hundred dollars to his bigger ones.

Life was good. He was doing what he wanted to do. He was having great sex with a smart and sometimes funny woman. He had his dog, and he lived in a town that had given him unexpected opportunities. He'd insisted on paying Blake rent, and between his disability compensation and the sales of his lighting fixtures, he was even putting money in the bank.

"This is a perfect day," he said.

"Sure it is," Blake said. "But I can tell it's not because of the fish you're not catching. You know that just about everyone in town knows you're getting shagged, don't you?"

Wes's pole jerked, but he ignored it, staring at his uncle. "The *whole* town?"

Blake grinned. "People live across the street from you and Hayley, and they have windows. I think a few have binoculars, too."

Wes groaned.

"They're like Santa here," Blake continued. "Though they may not see you when you're sleeping, they see you when you're sneaking over to her house, then sneaking back to your place before her mom comes home."

Wes was quiet for a moment. "So, they must know about you and Susan, too."

"Probably, but they don't care about us. The younger ones hope they'll still be sneaking around and doing it at our age. And the older residents are living vicariously through us, hoping the same miracle will happen to them."

Wes glanced at him. "You're not *that* old."

"Thank you." His uncle's voice was dry. "That's reassuring."

Wes felt another jerk on his rod, but he ignored this one, too. "It's not all about sex."

"You say that because you're still young. It's always about sex."

"You're still in your prime."

"My prime was in my twenties. Not my teens when I was too fast and too eager. Once I hit my twenties, I was able to slow down and enjoy it more." Blake grinned. "The ladies enjoyed it more, too.

Right now I'm at the age where I relish every encounter. If I'm lucky, I'll keep going until I'm in my nineties."

"A little too much information. Up till now, it was a good day."

Blake chuckled. "I'm just warning you to appreciate what you've got. Is it serious?"

Wes didn't answer right away, and his uncle didn't push him, remaining silent. Wes could hear the rustle of wind in the trees, Spock's breathing, and the sound of a car driving down the back road. A few small boats were out on Lake Michigan, too far away to tell if it was someone they knew or tourists.

"Right now," he said slowly, "the only thing I'm serious about is fishing. Yes, I have a girlfriend, but we wanted to keep it on the down low."

Blake snorted a laugh.

"And I have a dog." Wes looked down at Spock dozing beside him, then glanced at his uncle. "And you, too. You made this all possible."

"If I can't share my home with my favorite nephew, what good am I?"

"The best. That's what you are. You're like Mom that way."

"She was truly the best."

Wes sniffed and nodded, then waved his hand in the air, encompassing the lake, the cabin, the town, his uncle, his woman. "And all this might change in an instant, so for now, I'm just savoring the good parts."

"Savoring? Like food?"

Wes set the fishing rod across his thighs, not even pretending to fish anymore. "Remember when you invited me to live here? You told me it would be dull in Trouble Bay."

His uncle grinned. His fishing rod curved downward, but if he had a bite, he was ignoring it, too. "I didn't lie, but life never stays the same. Life is usually good here. Usually peaceful, especially at night. But even then, without any notice, fireworks will sometimes light up the sky like it's the Fourth of July."

"I suppose you're right," Wes said. "No matter what we do, there always seems to be a few surprises. Like the desks you're making with a hidden drawer."

"What are you getting at?"

"Hayley and her mom."

Blake raised his eyebrows.

"We talked about them lying about living in Chicago. Now I'm curious to know *why* they lied. I want to know what they're hiding. Or who they're hiding from."

His uncle was still for a moment. Wes listened to the sounds of the lake. The birds. A car driving down the road in front of the cabin.

"You want to be their white knight?" Blake asked.

"More like a battered knight."

"I have to admit that I'm curious, too. I wonder if Susan and her daughter are on the run from someone. Maybe an ex." Blake got to his feet. "I'm giving up fishing for the day. Guess I'm not in the mood. Susan's probably still in the workshop. I'll check to see if she needs any help."

Wes got to his feet more slowly as his uncle gathered his gear. Waking up from his nap, Spock jumped up. Wes bent to pet Spock behind his left ear. Hayley's past wasn't any of his business, but if she and the baby were in danger, he was going to make it his business.

He was trained to protect. It was in his blood now. In his heart. Maybe he was damaged and he couldn't save the world, but he was still functioning. He could still protect one woman in particular. And her baby, too.

He swung his rod over his shoulder and closed the tackle box, then walked down the pier to the sloped hill behind his uncle's house and up to the covered front porch. The ground was uneven, and he concentrated with every step.

Spock watched him the whole time. Another dog would be watching the skies for birds or the backyard for rabbits or other animals to chase. Not Spock, the best dog in the town. Maybe the best dog in the world.

"I'm going to wash up." Blake turned toward his house.

Wes headed to the shed a few minutes later, stashing his tackle box inside. Then he glanced at Spock. "Want to visit Hayley?"

Spock barked eagerly.

"Want to visit Finn?"

Spock barked even louder. The dog loved the baby, and the baby loved him, too.

Wes had known a lot of people in his life, but he was pretty sure his dog was smarter than most of them. Better behaved, too.

As they walked away, he didn't know who was more eager to see Hayley, him or the dog. Probably him. Sex was a powerful incentive, and he wasn't ashamed to admit it.

IT WAS MID-DAY, and Hayley lay on her bed, a little sweaty and feeling wanton. She smiled up at the ceiling, then turned her head to the man lying next to her. "Well, that was pretty..." She stopped and exhaled as Wes turned toward her.

His chest wasn't heaving anymore, and neither was hers. But just minutes ago, grunts and exclamations and a few callings to God were coming out of both their mouths.

He turned his head. "Pretty what?"

"Wonderful."

He smiled slowly. "Wonderful for me, too."

She smiled back. It felt as if there was a ball of sunshine inside her chest. Who knew she would be so happy in this small Wisconsin town? With a baby and a lover? None of this felt like it was real, but right now she didn't give a whoop.

This was her in-between life. Her transition time. Sex for the sake of sex. Not expecting anything more than carnal enjoyment.

This wasn't like her. She'd always been so serious. But not now.

Now she was in this never-never land, and the odd thing was that she liked it. No expectations. No obligations. Except for the baby and taking care of the bookkeeping and the website for her mother, Wes, and Blake.

Okay, maybe she couldn't entirely shove off her sense of responsibility like it was an old skin she no longer needed. But this sexual fling was working really well for her.

From Wes's grin, it was working for him, too.

She leaned over and kissed him. A big, long, wet kiss. Pushing up, she said, "Thank you. It was a nice surprise."

"Anytime."

She grinned and started to turn away.

He reached out, his hand on her arm stopping her. "You know that your mother has been sleeping over at my uncle's lately?"

She raised her eyebrows. "Yes."

"You said that Finn's been sleeping well in the smaller bedroom by himself."

She nodded.

"I've never slept over with you and had breakfast with you. I'd like to do that."

There was silence as an ache started inside her. Her mother always said she overthought things. That she needed to follow her heart.

But in this case, she wouldn't be following her heart; she would be following her libido.

Funny, all these years of being the sensible one—the girl who always did the right thing—and look where that had gotten her. In the witness protection program, living in a one-story ranch in a small tourist town. Not just her, either. She was sharing the house with her mother and her baby.

Why not be a little crazy for once? Why hold back?

"I suppose we could do it," she said slowly.

"Tonight?"

"Again?"

He nodded.

"If my mother sleeps over with your uncle, then, yes. Tonight would be fine." Her heart was beating faster, and she laughed out loud. Immediately feeling better. Maybe being a little crazy was the best medicine for her. For once in her life, she wasn't worrying about the rightness or wrongness of what she was doing, or what other people thought about it.

After all, the worst had already happened. No one was going to look for her here in a small vacation town. This was a new life, and she was a new woman. This new woman was going to loosen up and enjoy herself, and that was that.

24

"I GOT IT."

Listening to Yuri's matter-of-fact words, Polina clenched her prepaid cell phone in her hand. The one that no one knew she had but Yuri. She sat on the balcony of her home. It was June already. Two weeks since she'd talked to her mother-in-law. Two weeks since she'd sent money to the woman and her son. Money that would maybe save a child.

And maybe give her one.

Or not.

A stiff wind was blowing at her face, her eyes watering. She turned away from the wind and the view of the oceanfront and the yachts. Everything she'd once thought she'd wanted.

Now she felt stifled. The fairy tale had turned into a nightmare. Though her mother-in-law wasn't quite the witch she'd been before, she couldn't say that Leo had turned into a prince. On her visit yesterday, he'd blamed her for his incarceration and the loss of his baby. *His baby*.

It never was going to be hers.

His change of attitude hadn't surprised her. He was like that. If something went wrong, he blamed others.

She could see her future if she didn't take action soon. In a casket, lowered into the ground. And when she glanced around, there weren't many mourners around to see her off.

Perhaps she was exaggerating, but worry and her own inner conflicts and regrets were impossible to ignore.

She knew what she needed to do. Knew what was the right thing to do. She'd been in denial for too long. It was time she snapped out of it.

And then there was the black car parked on the street outside her house, just a short distance away. Too far away for her to see the two men sitting in them. But when she'd driven away from home two days ago, the black car had followed her ... all the way to the prison and back.

She missed going to Yuri's house, but she liked breathing and staying alive more than she liked great sex.

"You have the new identity card?" she asked.

"Yes. You're sure you want to do this?"

"Don't ask me that again. It makes me wish you were here so I could hit you."

Yuri laughed. "Or make love to me?"

She sighed. "'Fraid not. I think I should leave as soon as possible."

There was silence for a few seconds before he spoke again. "You're going to retrieve the baby?"

"Retrieve it? Like a dog retrieves a newspaper?"

He didn't say anything, and neither did she. She couldn't. Not with the tears pooling in her eyes.

"Are you all right?"

She sniffed and swiped the tears away. "Of course I am."

There was another few seconds of silence. "What about the baby? Don't you want the address?"

"I don't know what baby or what address you're talking about."

"Are you *sure* you're okay?"

"As sure as I can be. As sure as I've been in a long time. I was a little crazy for a while. I'm not so crazy anymore."

He chuckled softly. "You're an amazing woman."

"I know, but thank you." More tears wanted to fill her eyes and she willed them to stop.

"So, where should we meet? The airport? A boat?"

"A shopping mall." She'd been planning this for days now. "The huge one with the aquarium. If anyone follows either of us, it won't be easy to find a parking spot near my car. We can meet by the bookstore on the second floor. You should park on the north side."

"Sounds like a good plan."

"Don't look for a redhead. Look for me wearing a short brown wig and a Wonder Woman T-shirt." And money in her purse. Enough money to fly to an island where the music was sweet and the ocean waves lapped against the shore.

"No one will expect you to be wearing a Wonder Woman T-shirt," he said.

"That's what I thought. You should wear a disguise, too."

"I'll wear my Miami Marlins cap."

She rolled her eyes. Why was everything easier for men? She had to wear a wig. He only needed a cap.

"What day?"

"Saturday." She'd already purchased tickets under the new identity that Yuri had bought for her. "The mall is busiest on a Saturday. It will be harder for them to find us. The stores have the early bird sales. We'll meet at ten a.m."

He agreed, and they hung up. She strode into the house, closed the patio door, then hurried down the long hallway to her bedroom, beginning her preparations. Gathering her tote, her duffel bag, her wig, her jewelry, three changes of clothes, and twenty-eight thousand dollars, which was all she had left after paying off the kidney donor.

Except for the ace up her sleeve...

This was the scariest thing she had done.

And maybe the dumbest.

And definitely the bravest.

She ran to the bathroom, because she had the feeling she was going to throw up.

THE WINDOWS WERE OPEN. Hayley's spirits were up. It was a beautiful day. Sunny and perfect. Right now—right this minute—Hayley's life seemed sunny and perfect, too. Sitting at her new writing desk in the living room, she looked at the numbers on the laptop and wished there was someone she could talk to. Someone she could share this with.

She turned to the playpen where Finn was playing with the rattle. "Guess what?" she asked.

"Gah!"

"We're making money!"

"Gah! Gah!" On his stomach, Finn wiggled toward her like an ungainly worm.

She got up and walked over to the playpen, looking down at him. "Your grandmother sold two chairs. Wes and Blake are selling their stuff. And I'm getting paid! It's not much yet, but I'm going to start saving for your college tuition. Isn't that wonderful?"

He spit. Drool slithered down his chin, and he gurgled a laugh. He kicked his legs out, trying to scoot over to her faster, but though his will was strong, his motor skills were weak.

"I can see you're going to be a sloppy kisser." She bent, then scooped him up and kissed him anyway before wiping drool off of her chin. Love beat drool, but then she was his mom. "The girls aren't going to like that. You'll probably want to take care of it by the time you're older."

He spoke a series of syllables and patted her face with his starfish hand.

A knock came from the front door. As she twisted around, the door opened.

Wes stepped inside, holding the door open for Spock.

"You scared me." She set Finn back in the playpen then put her hand over her chest and felt the fast beating of her heart. "I must have left the door unlocked when I, well—"

"Said good-bye to me this morning?" he asked.

"Yes. That." She shrugged. The neighbors already knew they were a couple. A *temporary* couple. And no one was shocked. Amused maybe. Titillated maybe. Nothing else.

"Maybe I should search for a peg leg," he said, "like Long John Silver. The *clump, clump, clump* would warn you."

"You'd do that? What a great idea." She grinned, happy that he could make a joke about his prosthetic leg.

He was so much like her. Damaged but surviving. Maybe that's why they'd clicked. Her mother thought she felt more for Wes than appreciation and lust, but Hayley didn't want to listen. Didn't want anything to ruin the most uncomplicated relationship she'd ever had. Just friends. Just sex. She and Wes were like two peas in a pod. Two wounded people helping each other heal.

Sexual healing. What could be wrong with that?

"You're back soon," she said. "The fish weren't biting?"

He shrugged. "My favorite part of fishing is sitting on the pier in the sunlight. I'm not really a fishing guy."

"What kind of guy are you?"

"A sex god. Isn't that what you called me last night?"

She snorted a laugh, and Finn laughed, too, his arms slashing the air.

Bending over the playpen, she kissed the top of his hair that smelled like baby shampoo. "Aren't you a smart baby? Yes, you are a smart baby."

"Takes after his mom," Wes said.

"I *hope* he takes after me." She picked up a stuffed bunny and wiggled it in front of Finn. He grabbed it, and one bunny ear fit just right into his mouth.

"Do you want to talk about his dad?" he asked.

Straightening, she switched her gaze to Wes and shook her head, her stomach muscles tightening. "There's not much to talk about."

"You don't want to talk in front of Finn?" he asked.

"We don't know what babies can understand." She shrugged, her happy mood muted. "Anyway, it's over. It was ... a bad time. A bad relationship. I never want to see him again. I never want him to see Finn. I want nothing to do with him or his family."

"Did he hit you?" His voice hardened.

"No. And let's not talk about him." She frowned. He didn't usually ask personal questions, but she knew he wondered about her and her mother. Wondered why they had settled in a place where they didn't know anyone. She knew he didn't buy the story that she and her mother had fled from Chicago to Door County because she wanted a small town life for herself and her baby.

The marshals had been wiser than they knew, though Hayley doubted they had set up an army veteran in the house next door for her enjoyment. Or his taller uncle for her mother. No, she didn't think that setting them up with sex partners would be in the US Marshals' instruction book.

"What are you thinking?" Wes asked.

"Something silly."

He smiled slowly. "I'd like to hear something silly."

"You would?" She grinned. Once again, he was distracting her from her thoughts. "Remember when we talked about the Marvin Gaye song 'Sexual Healing'? I was just thinking that sexual healing is working for me."

He stepped toward her. "Me, too."

She put her hand out to ward him off, laughing, feeling good now, as if she could float off into the clouds. "Not while Finn's awake."

"I can wait." His eyes were intense, and she shivered in the warm sunlight shining through the windows.

"I hope so, since we just had sex last night."

"That was yesterday. Before midnight. This is a new day. If it's too soon for you, then tell me."

"No! I like it soon." As soon as she said the words, she put her palms over warm cheeks. "Well, that was embarrassing."

He laughed, his eyes bright. "Not embarrassing for me. We're good together."

"It could be baby mama hormones." She made a face. "This is so odd for me. I've never felt like this before. I've never talked like this, either. It's so strange to come to Wisconsin, of all places, to find my perfect lover."

He grinned widely, and she groaned. "There I go again."

"Don't stop. I'm not complaining."

"I shouldn't have said that. I've always been ... a bit reserved. I've been accused of being unemotional. Maybe having a baby opened me up."

"Maybe it's because in different ways we've both been damaged." His eyebrows drew together. "Maybe you feel safer with me because of my leg—"

"Stop!" She stepped closer to him and put her hand on his shoulder. "Don't say that," she whispered fiercely. "You are more masculine than any other man I've been with. It's not about the leg, stupid. It's about the way you touch me. The way you kiss me. The way you look at me. The way—"

He reached out and pulled her against him. Holding her tightly against him, he kissed her thoroughly. She clung to him and moaned as the kiss went on. Still, he held her. Still, he kissed her. The heat inside her was rising, and he moaned again.

The front doorbell rang. They jerked apart, staring at each other.

Then Finn cried. Spock barked. She took another step away from him, her breathing fast. He swore under his breath.

"I'd better answer it." Hayley's voice shook. She felt heated and flustered. She looked down. Her clothes were okay—white shorts and a yellow T-shirt—but she'd felt naked during the kiss.

Well, not naked, actually, but she'd *wanted* to be naked.

She picked up Finn and handed him to Wes. "Take him to the kitchen, please. I'll be right back."

He took Finn from her, and the baby clung to his neck, his crying stopped, as if he knew he was safe in Wes's arms.

"Why do we have to leave?" Wes asked. "I'm your neighbor. A friend."

"We know we're friends, but almost everyone in Trouble Bay thinks that we're lovers."

"Friends and lovers."

She groaned. "We'll talk about it later."

He laughed softly, then held out Spock's leash. "Okay, I'll go, but only if you keep Spock with you."

She raised her eyebrows. Did he think she needed a guard dog? But she took the leash and watched him stride into the kitchen.

25

STEPPING INTO THE KITCHEN, WES REMEMBERED THE strain in Hayley's face and the tightening of her body—as if she were getting ready to run—when he'd asked about Finn's father.

She wasn't a woman who would scare easily, but she'd been scared.

He wondered who would be visiting her. And why?

Maybe he was making too much of it. Maybe it was a neighbor collecting money for the church. Maybe someone was selling cookies. Maybe someone wanted to set up an appointment for Hayley's mother to paint her furniture.

The front door opened, and Hayley said something, talking in a low voice, as if she didn't want him to hear her.

He scowled, not liking his thoughts that were close to paranoid. If Hayley was keeping something from him about Finn's father, that was her choice and none of his business.

"Has anything unusual happened since you've been here?" a woman said in the front room, her voice pleasant enough. Normal. Only the question wasn't normal. It was a psychiatrist's question. Or a doctor's.

Hayley replied, her words still not loud enough for him to hear.

He wasn't waiting here any longer. He stepped into the hallway, Finn's hot forehead pressed against the front of his throat. By the time Wes strode into the living room and stopped about a foot behind Hayley, Finn was fast asleep.

A tallish woman stared at him. Hayley turned, narrowing her gaze at him, giving him her evil-eye squint. She clearly would have preferred that he'd waited in the kitchen.

Spock rushed up to Wes, his tail wagging, his mouth open in a big doggy smile.

At least someone was happy to see him.

"Oh, there's the baby," the woman said, her voice pitching higher as she bent to stare into the baby's eyes. "I recognize the red curls. He's gotten so big since I last saw him."

"Um, Wes, this is Tracey." Hayley gestured at the woman. "She lives in, um—"

"Green Bay." The woman was about the same height as Wes. She wore navy blue pants suit that looked institutional, and her eyes zoned in on his leg, though most people couldn't tell he had a prosthesis and barely noticed that the hitch in his step. "You were in the service?"

"I was in the army," he said, foretelling Tracey's question before she voiced it.

"Thank you for your service," she said. "I'm the rental agent for this house. I was in the area and stopped to see how well it's going."

"Wes lives next door." Hayley handed him Spock's leash, then lifted Finn into her own arms. The baby made a soft noise as he leaned his head against her breasts. "Thanks for holding Finn. Oops. You need to put stain remover on your T-shirt. He dribbled something on it."

"No worries. I'll go home and let you two talk." He nodded at Tracey. "Nice to have met you."

She moved out of his way, her gaze sliding down to his prosthetic leg as he walked forward with Spock slightly behind him. He glanced at Hayley, and her cheeks were pink.

They should be. She was a lousy liar. He'd been in the military long enough to recognize an official figure when he saw one, despite her baby talk. Tracey wasn't a military officer, but he'd bet the money in his bank account that she was some kind of an authoritative figure. If he had to take a wild guess, he'd say US Marshal.

It was coming together. Maybe he'd read too many suspense books or watched too many thrillers, but he had an idea of what might be going on and why Hayley was so secretive. As he reached the end of the sidewalk and turned toward his house, he saw a sedan parked in front of the house.

It told him nothing. That was okay. His mind was putting two and two and another pair of twos together and was coming up with one conclusion.

"I SAW HIS DOG TAGS." Tracey's eyebrows rose. She sat on the recliner while Hayley sat on the couch next to her recliner. "He's a veteran. Disabled, I'd guess. It's his left foot. You and he are having an affair, aren't you?"

A sound came from the playpen, Finn having fun with one of his toys. Hayley glanced at him and saw he had his happy face on. Why not? He'd slept, peed, pooped, eaten, and drunk. He'd been cuddled by his mom and Wes. His face had been licked by Spock. Not a bad life.

He should be busy with his toys for a while, she thought, turning to Tracey.

"That's not your business," she said.

"I have to ask. Are you sure your neighbor isn't a plant?"

"He lived next door for months before we moved here. It's his uncle's house."

"He lives with his uncle?" Her left eyebrow raised.

"His uncle lives in a cabin by the lake now. About five minutes away. Before that, he lived next door for something like twenty years. He bought the cabin last year, planning on renting it out for the summer. But when he heard about Wes's injuries, he moved into the cabin and invited Wes to stay at the house."

"His uncle is one of the good guys." Tracey nodded approval. "So, you've known Wes since you moved in?"

"Soon after." Hayley's face warmed as she remembered standing nude in front of the bedroom window, her breasts full with milk.

Since then, he'd seen her naked more times than she wanted to count, so she didn't know why she still blushed. It wasn't as if Tracey could read her mind.

"What's Wes's last name?" Tracey took out her phone, ready to tap his name in.

Hayley spelled his surname for Tracey. Then Tracey asked for his uncle's name. After Hayley told her Blake's full name, she added she and her mother were in business with Wes and Blake, summarizing their different specialties.

"You should have told me that right away." Tracey gave her a hard look.

"We just started. At this point, we aren't sure if we're going to continue. It depends on how profitable it is. My mother is confident that it will work out, but she's always optimistic. I'm more cautious. This business is in the trial-and-error stage. And I'm wondering what will happen when tourist season is over."

Tracey's eyebrows rose. "You really are cautious. Are you making money yet?"

"My mother is doing very well. Not just with tourists, but with locals, too. Considering the time we put into this, she's not making a lot yet. She thinks it will improve as more people know about her. We're still learning her market. We've already discovered that couches don't sell well for tourists. They're too big and bulky for tourists to transport home. Mom is focusing on smaller chairs for the summer crowd. So my answer to your question is that we hope it will get better."

Tracey frowned. "You'll be reporting your earnings?"

"Of course. Oh, and my mother repainted these two reclining chairs." She gestured at the recliner Tracey was sitting on, and the one she was sitting on. "I think they look amazing."

"I noticed them right away. Very nice." Tracey leaned back and raised the footrest. "This is amazingly comfortable. I have an ugly recliner that my ex never bothered to pick up after I kicked him out. It's been seven years now."

"Have you considered giving it to a place like Habitat for Humanity? Or a halfway house near your home?"

"I could, but the chair is almost as comfortable as this one. It's just an ugly color."

"I'm sure my mother would paint it for you for nothing."

"That's against regulations."

Hayley shrugged. "You can find videos that will show you how to do it."

"I've never been good with a paintbrush. I could ask my daughter. She's in her third year of college, and I'm helping her pay for it. She's going into pharmaceuticals. That's where the real money is, you know."

"And the real crooks."

"Pharmaceuticals *and* politicians. But don't tell anyone I said that." She grimaced. "Well, good luck to your mom. I like the light green. It would look good in my living room, too."

"I can email you links that my mother used."

"My daughter can find anything on the Internet. If she doesn't want to paint the recliner, she'll find someone else to do it. And I'm glad things are going well for you. Remember not to share anything that happened in Miami with your new guy."

"I hadn't planned on it. Have you heard anything new about Leo or his wife?"

"Not a thing. Normally, the only news we hear is bad news. So no news is good news."

Hayley nodded, but she didn't completely believe that theory. No news might mean Leo's wife or parents were outsmarting the US Marshals.

"I can see you worrying," Tracey said. "The system you're in is called the United States Federal Witness Protection Program for a reason. That's what we do. Protect you."

Hayley nodded. She knew that, but it was still hard to forget that people wanted to kill her.

"I won't forget to check on your neighbor and his uncle," Tracey added.

"Wes and Blake were here long before we moved in," Hayley said. "They were both in the military, too."

Tracey leaned frowned and turned toward her. "You're probably right, but I get the feeling that it's a case of the lady protesting too much. What are you afraid of?"

Hayley opened her mouth to refute her, but no words came out.

"You're worried that you might be conned again." Tracey looked straight into her eyes. "After what happened in Miami, I can't blame you. My son's in the army, so I could be prejudiced, but what if, instead of your worst fears happening, your greatest hopes and dreams happen instead?"

Hayley stared at her. Inside her chest, she felt something tighten. She was pretty sure it was her heart.

Tracey lowered her footrest and pushed off of the recliner with a sigh. "If I find anything on your neighbor or his uncle, I'll let you know. I'm sorry your mother's not here, but I'm guessing that wherever she is, she's doing just fine."

"That's my mom." Hayley got to her feet, too. "Doing just fine."

"I believe you'll do just fine, too. I like both of you, but you're more complex than she is. You think too much." Tracey tapped her right index finger against her forehead. "Sometimes it's easier to go with the flow."

"My mother doesn't go with the flow," Hayley said. "She *is* the flow."

Tracey laughed and headed to the front door. Hayley watched through the screen door until Tracey got into her sedan and drove away.

Hayley closed and locked the front door. Probably nothing bad was going to happen. Not here anyway. But she was cautious by nature, and she had a baby to protect.

Everything in her life seemed to be still changing, still turning upside down. She had a baby. She had a lover. She'd actually felt a bond with Tracey today. She lived with her mother and her baby son in a place she'd never heard of before—and if she had, she would never have felt the urge to visit. And now she was in charge of the business end for three unusual artists.

Her list of novelties was growing.

Her cell phone rang, and she hurried to pick it up, seeing her mother's name on the screen. She put it to her ear as she glanced at Finn. He was trying to put a large red and blue plastic ball in his mouth.

"Hi, darling," her mother said. "Guess what?"

"You know I'm bad at guessing." Hayley wondered if she should take the ball away, but decided not to. She washed his rubber and plastic toys once a week. It shouldn't be too germy.

"Blake is taking me to a shooting range. Would you like to come with us? We talked about this before but never got around to it. I have a babysitter lined up."

"I don't know—"

"She's very reliable. A lot like you, from what I hear. She's fifteen and babysits for quite a few neighbors."

Hayley put her hand on her forehead. She'd wondered what would be next, and here it was. "Sure, why not?"

"That's what I always say," her mom said, her tone happy. "You're getting to be like me."

Hayley held back a groan.

"I'll call the babysitter. Her name is Tori. When she gets here, walk over to Wes's. He's coming, too. He'll take you to the shooting range." Susan laughed. "This is going to be fun."

She hung up, and Hayley frowned. Susan was wrong. Learning the basics of shooting a gun was *not* going to be fun for her. Learning how to shoot a gun just made sense. It was a precaution. It wasn't likely to happen, but what if Leo's people were looking for the baby? What if they showed up to take Finn from her?

Even if they had to die doing it.

Or if they had to kill doing it.

Of if *she* had to kill to stop them.

She would much prefer the first option. If not, then she wouldn't hesitate to take the third option.

26

OLGA STOOD INSIDE HER HUSBAND'S OFFICE THAT could have been created for a king.

But all she saw was a murderer. A killer of her dreams and hopes.

"You're sure Polina is gone?" Olga looked at her husband with his lined face and his eyes that were nearly black. They'd never loved each other, but for a long time she had believed they respected each other. He was in charge of his Russian Mafia the same way that Russian kings and queens had ruled their country in earlier centuries. By strength. By ruthlessness. By killing anyone who was in their way.

Compassion is for fools, Peter liked to say.

The first time Olga had heard him say that, she'd been a young woman with a body like a porn star, an average face, and a brain like a criminal mastermind.

She'd loved another man. Passionately.

Her ancestors had been Russian royalty. Even after they were stripped of their titles, they still did well because they had two skills. They killed people. They slept with people.

Sometimes they even married people, but only if they were very, very rich. Or very, very powerful.

From the beginning, she had known Peter would cheat on her. That was a given. But she hadn't expected him to be so blatant in his womanizing.

It was no wonder their only son turned out to be a man whore. The Prince of Fools.

He took after his father that way.

"She's flown the coop," Peter said. "I know you've been talking to her lately. What did she say?"

She stared at him, knowing the stoniness in her face and eyes matched the stoniness in her heart. She'd suspected that Peter had a secret yen for her daughter-in-law with her redheaded beauty, her swimsuit-model body, and her husky laugh. Men were stupid that way.

She was also sure that Polina despised Peter.

"She wants to find the baby." Olga had to tell him that much. He probably already knew it. "She hired Yuri Petrov to find him. He told her it was a waste of her money, but she wanted to try."

"Was that all?"

"No. She was depressed."

"You know that Yuri probably fucked her."

She stiffened, suspecting he was angry because Yuri had succeeded where he'd failed. "Leo cheated on her."

"She knew about it. She agreed."

"You know that the woman wasn't the first one."

He narrowed his eyes. "Are you defending her? Now that Leo is in prison, do you think their marriage will last?"

She raised her chin. "You tell me. What do you think?"

Her husband looked at her, his face impassive, and a chill went through her. She knew about his other children. His two daughters. She knew he was seeing other women now. More than one. Maybe one of them was pregnant. Maybe he would have another child, and this one would be a boy.

The chill in her bones grew colder.

"If you value your life," he said, "you should leave right now."

"Peter, I—"

"Enough." He sliced his hand at the air, like he was holding a sword. "Out."

"Peter—"

He looked at her, and in his eyes, she saw hatred.

Her breath sucked in. She got to her feet, feeling sick. Without a word, she turned and walked out of his office. As she did, she imagined her life crumbling in pieces around her.

POLINA STRODE AWAY from her car parked in the middle of the second row in the mall's east parking lot, her calf-leg sundress swishing against her thighs. The blue tote bag was heavy on her shoulder, but she walked as if it were empty. No one seemed to be following her, but she wasn't taking chances.

Halfway through the mall, she headed into a bathroom, going to the handicapped stall at the end of the row of toilets.

It took her a minute to change her sundress for a short tan skirt and a Wonder Woman top. In another minute, she stepped out of her pricey sandals and into a pair of sneakers. Quickly, she pulled a rolled up duffel bag from the bottom of the tote, then shoved the tote, sandals, shorts, and black top into the larger duffel bag.

Last, she put on a wig.

Everything set now, she stepped out of the stall and headed to the mirror. Looking at her reflection, she saw a woman with short brown hair and black-rimmed glasses wearing a Wonder Woman T-shirt. The woman looked attractive in an average way.

The wig was slightly longer on the left than the right. Polina adjusted it, then turned and walked out the side exit, different from the one she'd entered. She immediately spotted a dark-haired man in his thirties wearing charcoal-gray pants and a blue shirt. Leo's second-in-command. Her nerves on alert, she passed her gaze over him as if he were nothing. Forcing herself not to hurry, she turned toward the escalator that led to the second floor.

Nearing the top, she glanced down. He was still sitting on the bench, staring at the women's bathroom entrance.

She turned away, her heart pounding.

It was still pounding when she reached the bookstore and saw a man wearing khaki pants and a Marlins cap lean against the brick wall. He looked like someone's bored husband waiting for his wife. When he saw her, he straightened.

She wanted to laugh out loud, but instead she only grinned. Reaching him, she said, "Let's blow this joint."

He took her hand, and they headed toward the next exit.

They didn't talk until they were outside and striding down a row of cars. "You made it," he said.

She squeezed his hand. It could still go wrong. She wouldn't allow herself to relax until she was on the plane that would take her to her brand new life.

"Here." He tugged her toward a boxy brown car.

"This doesn't look like a car you'd drive."

"It's a friend's car." He pressed a remote, then opened the passenger door. "Get in."

"You thought of everything," she said when he slid into the driver's seat and closed his door. "My new passport and new identity. I don't know how you did it, and I don't want to know."

"I have friends in low places." He winked at her, then he started the car. "And I have even better friends in high places."

She nodded, peering around the crowded parking lot. Not seeing anyone she recognized. "We should get out of here."

He backed up, and they were on their way.

They didn't talk much until they reached the airport, only a twenty-minute drive from the mall. One of the reasons she'd chosen it. He parked by the terminal number she gave him. All she had was her duffel and her biggest purse, but he got out of the car and walked around to the passenger side by the curb.

They hugged. A long hug. Their mouths met, and her heartbeat accelerated.

After a long minute, she pulled back a few inches. He remained where he was.

"I'm proud of you," he said as people hurried past them.

"The truth is, I'm proud of myself." She beamed at him. "*I did it.*"

"You sure did."

"I'm going to be a free woman. My own woman."

He smiled, but there was a sadness in his eyes. "I'll miss you."

"I'll miss you, too."

"I wish I could go—"

"No." She put her fingertips over his lips. "Miami is your home. Your city. You love it here. I won't take you away from it."

"And you're not ready for another relationship, are you?"

"Honestly? If you could go with me, I wouldn't stop you. You're hard to resist."

"All the girls say that."

They laughed, and she cupped her hand on the side of his face. "It's the truth. There aren't many men like you."

"Or women like you. I don't know where you're going—"

"And I'm not telling you," she said.

He put his hand over hers. "You're going to do just fine. For what you did for that little boy, God and his angels have to be on your side."

She slipped her hand out from under his. "It was already a done deal. I didn't have any choice. Don't make me into a heroine."

"Bullshit. You could've said no. That transplant took all of your money, didn't it?"

"I have some left. Enough. And you know what I have in that bag?" She gestured at the duffel bag hanging on her back.

"Don't tell me it's gold bars," he said.

She grinned. "That would be too easy. It's jewelry worth at least twenty thousand. Maybe more. I won't be broke."

"You'll only get a fraction of the price."

"I'm getting my freedom. I'm getting a new life. That's worth a lot more than money."

"Why didn't you go to the Feds, like Leo's baby mama did?"

"She got to them before I did, and I don't know enough for them to protect me. Leo didn't talk about his other dealings to me. Besides, I think I'll do better by myself."

He still watched her face, and she felt the heat of hot tears in her eyes. She blinked hard. She didn't want to cry. Not now. Not for a long time.

"I need to go now. Don't feel sorry for me. I don't want your pity. I'm starting a new life, and I'm excited about it. This one is going to be all about *me*, not a husband with the personality of a spoiled toddler. And the money for the boy…" She shook her head. "Maybe that's my atonement for not trying to stop Leo from using that woman. For blaming her for his sins. For being selfish."

"You have a brave heart."

"And you have to leave."

He nodded, started to turn … then turned back.

"Go!" She pointed at the car. "Go now. I need to start my new life."

"If you ever need me..."

As she nodded, she knew she would never call him, never write him. She would probably never see him again.

Taking a deep breath, she walked away, resisting the temptation to look back at him. She felt a little sad, but that didn't last as she headed into the airport and hummed a happy song. Happy to leave Miami. Happy because of something that no one would know until Leo was out of prison. Something she hadn't mentioned to Yuri.

Leo had a safe in his office that he'd thought no one knew about.

He was wrong. She'd known. One day a couple years ago, she'd decided to surprise him and hang a framed photo of her and him in his office. When she took down the ugly picture he had on the wall, she discovered the hidden safe. She'd stared at it for a long moment, then returned the original picture over the safe, and she'd put their photo on his desk.

The safe had a combination that he'd probably thought no one would break.

Four days ago, it had taken her only four tries to open it.

Inside the safe had been eight hundred thousand dollars and a gun.

She'd left the gun in the safe. The money went straight to her tote bag, which was now in the bottom of her duffel bag.

Life was going to be wonderful. This was just the beginning.

27

"I NEED YOUR ADVICE." WES STOOD IN HIS UNCLE'S workshop, Spock at his side. Blake's furniture took up more space than Wes's lighting fixtures, so Wes was sharing his work area with Susan. Her pieces were bigger than his, but she had less inventory than Blake, whose space held a dozen different projects: a few bassinets that could be converted to cribs, wine racks that could also be used as shelving units, and coffee tables with storage areas. Focusing on items that had more than one function, and smaller items that might fit in tourists' cars.

"Advice about your lighting designs?" Blake set down his protective goggles and stepped away from the table saw.

"I'm thinking of trying different metals," Wes said. "Maybe I'll play with it in the winter. Right now, my lights are selling better than I expected. Not just for kids, either. Adults seem to like them, too."

"We're all kids at heart." Blake pulled a handkerchief out of his pocket and wiped wood dust off of his face. "Using plastic parts from old toys was an inspired idea. Gives you a nice profit."

"I'm feeling good about it, but that's not why I'm here."

"Let's go to the office and get some water. I need to get away from the wood dust."

Wes followed his uncle to the small room by the workshop entrance. It had a sink, a counter, a small fridge, and a microwave. There was one table, four metal folding chairs that were probably as old as Wes, and one bathroom. The cement floor was bad for Spock to sit or lie on for too long. After the first day that Wes and Spock had worked at the workshop, he'd driven to Sturgeon Bay and bought a large doggy bed that Spock settled onto now.

Blake got two bottles of water out of the fridge, handing one to Wes. They both sat at the round tile table in the unadorned industrial space and took big gulps of water. The cold liquid felt good going down Wes's throat.

After taking one last swallow, Blake set his bottle on the table. "Let me guess why you're here. You want to marry Hayley, right?"

"We met less than two months ago."

"Love doesn't follow a time schedule." Blake grinned. "Love is two people who fit together the way your prosthesis"—he gestured at Wes's prosthesis—"and your knee fit together."

"That's the worst comparison I've ever heard."

Blake laughed. "Yeah. It is pretty bad."

"You're not talking about me, are you?" Wes narrowed his eyes. "You're talking about yourself. You're falling for Susan, aren't you?"

"She's a beautiful woman, inside and out. She's smart and funny and talented." Blake shrugged. "What man wouldn't fall for her?"

Sitting back, Wes stared at his uncle. Right from the start, he'd thought that Susan and Blake were two of a kind, but he'd never expected his uncle to be serious about any woman.

"Don't get any ideas. I like her. A lot. She delights me. She makes me laugh. She makes me feel..." Blake took a deep breath. "Not young, I don't delude myself that I'm younger. Just happy to be alive." He rubbed his hand over his chin. "But I'm not looking for marriage. I don't think she is, either. I've been divorced twice already. Both wives said I was selfish and impossible to live with, and I took them for granted. They weren't lying. I'm just not good at lasting relationships."

"Apparently that's something you and Susan have in common."

"If I were a number," Blake said, "I'd be the uncommon denominator. I think Susan would say the same thing about herself."

"You and Susan aren't denominators. You're people."

"Like an old song says, 'people are strange.'"

"True. But you and Susan aren't old songs."

"We're *all* an old song," Blake said. "The history of the world is in old songs."

"All of us? What if I want to make a new song?"

"Is *that* why you're here? To talk about *your* new song? A new love? A new life?"

Wes frowned. "I'm going to tell you something that's just between you and me. You can't share it with anyone."

Blake nodded, his expression serious.

"I'm holding you to your promise to keep this to yourself."

Blake leaned closer to Wes.

"We're both sure that Susan and Hayley didn't come from Chicago. I think I know why they're lying."

"They're hiding from someone?" Blake asked. "An abusive boyfriend? My guess is the baby's father. It has to be Hayley. Susan's too independent and confident to be with someone abusive. Hayley's smart and independent, but she doesn't have her mother's self-confidence. She could be fooled by a guy who sweet-talked her. Who made her feel special. Who was hiding his true nature."

Wes's muscles tensed. On the floor, Spock raised his head, and Wes could see the tautness in Spock's body, too. He was reacting to Wes's tightened nerves.

Forcing his muscles to relax, Wes inhaled and then exhaled before he spoke again. "I think Hayley and Susan are in the witness protection program. I was there this morning when a woman stopped in wearing a bad pair of navy pants. She said she was the rental agent, but she sounded official to me. It's my guess that she's a US Marshal."

"You're basing your conclusion on ugly pants?"

"I'm basing it on the way they looked at each other, as if they were keeping a secret. And before the agent realized I was there, I overheard her asking if anything unusual had happened since they'd moved to Trouble Bay."

"She could've been talking about the house," Blake said.

"The house wasn't mentioned."

"Or you could be right," Blake said slowly.

A moment of silence passed, both of them frowning.

"If you asked Susan," Wes asked finally, "do you think she'd tell you the truth?"

"It's obvious she doesn't want to talk about it, so I don't want to push her."

"Maybe you should."

Blake just looked at him, still frowning, not giving anything away.

"I'm going to keep a close eye on them," Wes said.

"If they're in witness protection, they should be okay."

"They should." Wes looked down at his left leg, the one with the prosthesis. "But not everything turns out the way it should."

"I don't know what else we can do." Blake took another slug from his bottle, twisted the top back on, then stood. "If you get any ideas, let me know. I've got your back."

"I know you do." He stood, and so did Spock.

"You're going back to Hayley now, aren't you?" Blake asked.

Wes nodded.

"You think she'll tell you anything?"

"Doubt it. I'm not going to ask."

"Yet you're going over there." Blake shook his head. "You've got it bad."

"See you later." Wes turned. He disagreed with Blake. He didn't have it bad, he had it good. Every minute he spent with Hayley was good. Even when she was changing diapers.

He remembered the anger he'd felt when he was in the hospital. He'd been furious at pretty much everything, including himself for not letting the past go. For not healing mentally. For falling into a depression. For not climbing out of that deep, murky pit fast enough.

Blake had saved him. Inviting him to live in his house. Inviting him to work with him. Helping him create his light fixtures, though their ideas were so different.

And he had Spock. So much more than just a dog, Spock was his friend, his companion, his crutch.

Wes might be missing a part of his limb, but so were a lot of people. He was one of the lucky ones. There was no way he should feel sorry for himself.

His mind had told him those things, yet the darkness had lingered. A black cloud that wouldn't drift away to let the full sunshine in. Nothing had shoved that damn cloud out of him until the first time he'd looked out his window and seen the woman next door.

His staring had never been about her breasts. Not really. All women had breasts. It was her reaction that had made him want to laugh. Then more changes—more light—came from talking to her. The tenderness on her face as she held Finn. Listening to her matter-of-fact pronouncements.

And maybe it was her breasts a little. No other breasts. Only hers.

Everything led to her. Everything good.

"I'll talk to you later," he said, feeling light-headed. Almost giddy.

His uncle grinned. "Have fun."

Wes didn't answer as he stepped outside into the perfect June day, with the beginning of humidity, and the sun shining down on his face. He waited until Spock padded out of the workshop before he shut the door.

"Hayley saved me," he said to Spock, who looked up at him, his ears perked, his brown eyes focused on him with total attention, as if he were soaking in every word. "Now I'm going to make sure that if she needs saving, I'll have her back."

Spock opened his mouth and then barked. His way of saying, *I'm in, too.*

28

SUSAN OPENED THE SIDE DOOR AND STUCK HER HEAD IN the kitchen, where Hayley was slicing onions for the moussaka she was preparing for tonight's dinner.

"Come see the before!" Susan called out, then stepped back, the screen door flapping shut.

Hayley quickly washed her hands, wiped them on the dish towel, then checked to be sure that Finn was in the playpen in the living room. The windows were open. If he needed her, all he had to do was cry out.

That set, she hurried outside. Her mom was standing in the back of the silver van that Blake had loaned her. Both back doors were open. Her mother beamed at her.

Hayley slowed, her breath caught. They'd been in Trouble Bay for a little less than two months, and what a difference from their life in Miami. Her mother had been content in Miami selling real estate, but now she glowed. Hayley had never seen her like this. As if her mom had been three-fourths alive then, and she was fully alive now.

Hayley felt the same way, though she'd been the opposite of her mother, holding her emotions inside her. A watcher instead of a participant. Even when she'd dated Leo, she'd felt like an observer. Even during sex with him. She would think, *Yes, that's good.* Or, *Hmm, that's interesting, but I wish he would slow down. This isn't a race to see who finishes first.*

She would even rate her own moves by the loudness of his moans. If there had been an Olympic category for sexual performances, neither of them would have won any medals. They would've made it to contender status. Yet, even though she now knew why Leo had worked so hard to seduce her, she couldn't be sorry for it. Because of him, she had Finn.

Nor was she sorry her mother was beaming at her and gesturing at two brown chairs in the back of the van.

"Isn't this wonderful?"

Hayley made a face. "Mom, new ugly chairs? And these are brown, too."

"Yes, new chairs! And we've proved that ugly can be fixed. That's why this is so wonderful. When I'm finished with the chairs, you will look at them as if they're your favorite ice cream." Susan twirled around once, like a happy child. "I'm so excited about this. I'm creating something wonderful, and that makes me feel wonderful."

"I'm just glad you're happy here," Hayley said. "I know you loved your life in Miami, and I hated that you had to leave all your friends. I was afraid you'd be bored here. Afraid there wouldn't be anything interesting to do."

"Honestly," Susan said, "when we left, I was afraid, too. But now I'm happier than I ever was."

Hayley looked into her mother's eyes, unable to reply over the big knot in her throat. A breeze came from her left, and she smelled cut grass. She was aware of two neighbors chatting across the street to her left. At the end of the block, someone was pounding tiles on a roof. In Wes's yard, a squirrel climbed up the oak tree. And a blue car was coming down the street, driving slowly. Wes's car.

Her mother's gaze flicked to the road, and she smiled smugly. "Right now I'm seeing one fine reason for *you* to be happy."

As Wes's blue car turned into his driveway, Hayley felt a jump in her chest and a lump in her throat.

"I talked to your dad today." Susan raised her hand, as if to ward off any questions. "And don't worry. Both of us have the location tracking turned off. Plus, I called the number of the cell phone that Nancy gave him."

Hayley nodded. Nancy, her father's former paralegal, had retired a decade ago, but they'd remained friends. It was unlikely anyone would connect the cell phone Nancy had purchased under her mother's name and had given to her father.

"I told him about Wes," Susan continued, "and said I approve. After I described him, your dad said he approves, too."

Hayley's cheeks heated. "There's nothing to approve. Wes and I haven't talked about a future, and we might never talk about it."

Susan leaned forward to kiss her cheek, then hugged her before stepping back. "The thing is, honey, the future will take care of itself. I'm happy for you *right now*. So be happy for me right now, too. In the end, that's all we have."

"Mom, I'm not sure—"

"No one is sure, so stop worrying. Worry is a waste of time." Susan half turned toward the van. "I might be late tonight." She laughed. "Or I might not come home tonight. Don't wait up for me."

She hurried away, calling out a greeting to Wes, who was getting out of the car he'd parked by the curb, Spock jumping out after him. Wes waved to Susan, then switched his gaze to Hayley.

She stood straight, watching him stepping toward her. As her mother pulled the van away from the curb, he and Spock stopped a foot away from her.

"I just wanted to tell you that..." He stopped, looking worried.

Her heart pounded as he paused. Was he going to tell her that he *loved* her? Was that what was making him so nervous?

Through the years, a few men had avowed their love. She'd never said it back. Not even to Leo. Not that he'd noticed. He'd been too confident that any woman would love him to realize she'd never said it back.

Wes would notice.

She stared into his blue eyes. What would she say to him? Perhaps more important, what would he say to her?

"I think you're in the witness protection program."

Her mouth opened, but no words came out. Her thoughts were frozen.

"And I think I should move in with you."

WES SAW the shock in her eyes, then they darkened, and she snapped around and stomped to the house.

It wasn't what he'd expected. Maybe he'd been a little too blunt.

"Hayley, wait!"

She kept walking. He was aware that Norma and Wendy across the street had stopped talking, aware they were watching him and Hayley like hawks watched prey. He stepped stiffly after Hayley as he could and was only a couple of yards behind her when she stepped inside and slammed the door.

He knocked on the door. And knocked again.

He tried to turn the handle but nothing happened. She'd locked the door.

Spock barked.

He looked down, and Spock looked up. Wes could see in Spock's brown eyes his pity, as if the dog silently thought, *You screwed that up.*

"It ain't over yet," he said to Spock, then he turned and headed to his house.

29

HAYLEY PICKED UP FINN FROM THE PLAYPEN, THEN tiptoed to the side door and peeked out. Finn fussed in her arms, and she kissed his cheek.

Wes was gone. Stilling, she closed her eyes, then sighed and opened them.

This was what she'd wanted, wasn't it? And he'd given up easily. Obviously, she'd made the best decision.

Good, she told herself, heading back to the living room. She sat down on the recliner with Finn cradled in her arms, trying not to think, because all her thoughts were self-incriminatory. Finn sighed, his eyes closed, his mouth slightly open. Looking down at him, she told herself she should have taken a chance. Then she told herself she'd done the right thing.

A sound came from the side door. She stiffened. The sound came again, the screen door opening, and then the door.

Holding Finn tightly, she jumped up on her bare feet, her heart thumping. It wasn't her mom. She would have called out something like, "*I'm home.*" Her voice cheerful, as if she expected everyone to be happy to see her.

There was no cheer in Hayley's mind. Only fear and panic.

The gun. Where was her gun?

In the bedroom. But she and Finn were in the front room. Her cell phone was on the kitchen table. She swallowed. Still holding her sleeping son, she hurried into the hall toward her bedroom, her heart slamming inside her chest. Why hadn't she—

"Hayley."

Her breath stopped. *Wes.* Spock at his side. They stood in the hallway. In her panic and worry and unhappiness, she'd forgotten that she'd given him a key. She had keys for his place, too.

The truth was, she hadn't thought he'd come back after her rejection.

Looking at him, she saw he wasn't happy, his mouth a tight line, his eyes steely.

"You scared me," she said.

"I couldn't stay away. You're in trouble, aren't you? Let me help you."

"I can't. If I told you, and because of it, something happened to you..." She shook her head, her throat closing. There were no words for the way she felt. Only tears that she didn't want to spill out of her eyes.

He stepped toward her. "I know you, Hayley. No matter what name you're using, I know what you are. And I know *who* you are. You're a great mom, a great daughter, and—I'm not sure you want to hear this—a great lover."

Tears welled up in her eyes and she swayed as Finn made small sounds. "I could be trouble," she whispered.

"Don't you know? Anything can be trouble. I could walk across the street, and a speeding car could run over me. I could have a sudden heart attack. I could be struck by lightning."

"*None* of that will happen to you." She glared at him.

"I'm not immune." His voice was low. "I've lost so much already. I've lost half of my leg. I've lost people I've cared for." He paused, his gaze not leaving hers. "I don't want to lose you, too."

"How did you guess?" Her shoulders slumped. "It was Tracey, wasn't it? She looks like a ... well, a badly dressed US Marshal."

"Uncle Blake and I were suspicious long before I saw Tracey. We knew you and your mom aren't from Chicago. Your accents are all wrong."

"I don't have an accent!"

Smile lines creased his cheeks. "You do. It's not strong, but it's there. And you told us you came here while on vacation and fell in love with the town, but it was obvious neither of you knew anything about Trouble Bay or Door County."

She groaned. "We were told to read up on it. I normally would, but I'd just had a baby, my life had been torn apart, and I wasn't in a good place. And my mom was focusing on me and the baby. You know what she's like. If anyone asked questions, she probably thought she could charm away their doubts." She made a face. "It's my fault. I know better."

"Don't beat yourself up. It's not your fault, and we all have our secrets." He stepped closer to her and put his arms around her back. Then slowly and gently, he hugged her and Finn. His voice lowered to a husky murmur. "I'm pretty sure the whole town knows you're running from something."

"The *whole* town?" She craned her neck up to stare at his face. She felt stupefied. Or, more likely, she thought, just plain stupid.

"They probably think it's something to do with a man," he said.

She groaned. "That's even worse."

He chuckled. Sighing, she rested her head on his shoulder, with Finn cocooned between them. She had never been the type to lean on a man, but his shoulder felt so good beneath the side of her head. And his arms felt so good wrapped around her. Just this once, she was giving herself a pass to let someone else be strong for her.

They stayed like that for long minutes until Finn squirmed, making fussing sounds. She drew back, then Finn snuggled against her breast, his mouth open, his breaths even, his eyes closed.

"This little sweetheart is ready for a nap." She headed to the bassinet in the bedroom. When she laid him down, he cried out, his eyes half opening. She covered him with his blanket, then rubbed his shoulder. "Go to sleep," she whispered. "Mommy's here. So are Wes and Spock. We're all watching over you. You'll be just fine."

As if he understood her, his eyes closed, his head turned, a saliva bubble dribbled out of the side of his mouth, and he was asleep.

She padded out of the bedroom. Wes and Spock were waiting for her in the hall, and she led the way to the kitchen.

"Want to talk about it?" Wes asked.

"No." She went to the fridge and took out a pitcher of lemonade. Without asking him if he wanted any, she poured lemonade into two glasses and added ice. She set the glasses on the kitchen table, then took a seat while he sat down next to her. "Okay, I'll give you the short version of what brought us here. I was flattered when a handsome and wealthy businessman asked me out. He was in the process of a divorce. He didn't live with his wife. I checked him out online and didn't find out anything more."

He looked at her, not saying anything. No judgment in his face.

Her mouth was dry. She took a swallow of lemonade before continuing. "What my computer didn't know was that his father was the head of the Russian Mafia in Miami."

He sat taller, his body stiffening.

She held up her hand to stop him from saying anything. "What *he* didn't tell me was that his wife was having a hard time getting pregnant, and apparently I was a paler image of her."

"No." His voice was blunt and sure.

"Afraid so. It was a setup. He switched my birth control pills with look-alike placebos. I became pregnant very quickly. When I went to his place to tell him, I discovered texts between him and his wife. I found out what they'd done and who he and his family really were."

He looked at her, not saying anything. No judgment in his face.

"The short version is that I gathered some evidence against him and drove to my father's office." Seeing the slight frown on Wes's forehead, she said, "He's a lawyer. He took me to the US Marshals building in Miami. It took months, but I eventually testified against the creep in court. He's in prison now, and I'm in the witness protection program. They sent me here. Through the whole thing, my mother was with me. She insisted on coming to Trouble Bay with me and Finn."

"Anything else?"

She gazed into his eyes that looked back at her so seriously. "The marshals are confident that the Russian mob won't look for me here. Door County might be a big tourist spot in Wisconsin and neighboring states, but Florida has Disney World, the Florida Keys, the Kennedy Space Center, and so much more."

"It's still possible someone might discover your location."

"Anything is possible, but I've never heard of anyone from the Russian Mafia checking out Trouble Bay, Wisconsin."

He didn't reply, but she could see the worry in his eyes.

"I can't be constantly looking over my shoulder," she said. "I can't let fear run my life."

"Not fear," Wes said. "Caution. Don't you think if these people want the information badly enough they'll find a needy US Marshal to bribe? Someone desperate. Or someone with a family problem. People will do anything for family."

She stared at him, a sinking feeling in her belly. Leo wouldn't be able to search out someone like that. Not anymore. He was in prison. His only concern would be to save his own skin.

But what about his mother? Or father? Or his wife?

Were they desperate for her baby? The wife could want Leo's son. Leo's mother or father might want Finn, too.

Leo's wife ... she had been in the courtroom the first day that Hayley had testified. Hayley had recognized her from her photos on the Internet. Even from a distance, Hayley had seen the sadness on her beautiful face.

Leo's father had stayed away from the courtroom during the trial, but his mother had been there every day, her back straight, her chin high, her hair perfect, her face always made-up, her skin tight, reminding Hayley of a wicked Disney queen.

So different from Hayley's mother. If Susan was cast in a fairy tale, she would be the good fairy, sprinkling happy dust with a wave of her wand.

"If this were winter," Wes said, "we could spot a stranger in a second. We could keep watch on them. But tourist season is in full swing now. There are ten times more tourists than locals. If someone is looking for you, he could be anywhere."

"My mother said so many tourists were walking on Main Street over the weekend that they look like sardines."

"Sardines with money and credit cards."

She grinned, more comfortable now that the spotlight wasn't on her.

"You shouldn't take chances," he said, not letting her off the hook so easily. "You shouldn't be here alone with Finn."

"I'm not alone. I live with my mother."

"Your mother is spending most of her nights with my uncle. They're looking like a couple."

"My mother might spend nights with him, but I doubt it will go further than that. She likes being her own woman. She likes her freedom. She likes ... options. She doesn't like to be tied down to one man."

"She sounds like the female version of my uncle."

"She didn't *have* to move with me. I didn't ask her. It was her choice. She left the city that she loved for me and Finn. I can't kick her out of her bed in the house we share."

"You don't have to kick her out. She can live in her new house." He gestured in the direction of his place. "Right next door to you."

"I suppose you'll stay with me instead?"

"Yes."

"The whole town will talk."

"The whole town is already talking. You think they don't know about us?"

She looked away from him. Would it be horrible to have Wes live with her and Finn? Of course not.

The only horrible thing was that she might get used to him.

She might never want him to leave.

Sometimes when he sneaked away from the house early in the morning, she felt bereft by his absence. She missed him like she would miss a piece of her heart.

But what if he didn't feel the same? What if he *never* felt the same? What if he was just protective? And horny?

She turned back to him. "Probably nothing will happen, and now that you know my story, you're just freaking out a little. But there's a small possibility that you could be right, and I have to think of Finn. So, yes, I would appreciate it very much if you stayed with me and Finn. I just hope you won't be sorry."

"Don't you know?" he asked.

"Know what?"

He leaned toward her then kissed her. She melted against him. The kiss was long, and when he finally pulled back, she was breathless.

"I'm in love with you," he said.

She stared at him, emotion tumbling through her. Joy and fright were the strongest. In this second, this instant, it felt to her that just maybe she'd let fear run her life for too long. Or maybe she'd been in the wrong place, and now she was exactly where she was supposed to be. A small town with a small child and a small house ... and a man with a big heart.

Along with a mother with a big heart and a big personality.

Yet the soul-strangling fear was still there. Like a giant dark cloud, complete with lightning strikes, hovering above her head.

"I'll start packing," he said. Not waiting for her consent, he stood and walked to the side door.

She watched him leave, her mouth open.

This could be the best thing to happen in her life.

Or this could be the worst.

30

Olga looked up as Peter stepped into the room. She'd been trying to act normal, but nothing was normal anymore.

"What is it?" She looked out the window. It was early afternoon. He never returned home this early.

"Yuri claims not to know where Polina is. His friends swear he was with them all day. He was with another woman last night."

Her hands shook, and she clasped them together. Not saying anything, afraid that if she opened her mouth she would scream or cry or swear or grab the nearest items and throw them.

"I sent cars on every highway and expressway looking for her. I have people checking the airports and the cruise ships. Even boat rentals."

She gazed at him, raising her eyebrows. Still not saying anything.

He gave her an angry look, but she didn't flinch.

"How long has she been gone?" she asked.

"I don't know." He leaned forward. "You said you talked to her. Did she say anything to you? Mention a place where she'd like to live?"

"She said nothing like that." She looked at him calmly. "I have no clue where she might be."

He stared at her for a moment, then nodded his head sharply. "I came to inform you. Nothing more."

"Will you be back tonight?"

"I don't believe so," he said, then he turned and walked out into the hall. With each step, her head felt lighter. *Go*, she thought, *go and never come back.*

Finally, she stood and went to her private office across the hall that faced the driveway. Through the window, she watched his shiny black car in the front. About five minutes passed before he strode outside and slid into the backseat of his Rolls. She couldn't see inside the car, but she guessed his latest mistress was in it with him.

At church last Tuesday, her cousin—whose middle son was Peter's accountant—had whispered to her that Peter's twenty-three-year-old mistress had stopped taking her birth control pills. Per Peter's request.

The news had confirmed her fears. Her suspicions.

Peter had given up on Leo.

Maybe he was right to do so, though she blamed Peter for not reining Leo in much earlier. She'd tried, but Peter had treated him like royalty, letting Leo get away with, well, murder.

She hadn't replied to her cousin. Had only turned away.

Sometimes she felt that a block of ice had lodged in her heart.

She walked to the side of the library, staying off to the side of the window until she heard the car engine. A smooth sound, but her hearing was still good. Only after she heard the car drive away did she pull back a curtain and peer out the window, watching it until it was gone.

Enough.

She straightened and turned away. It was warm outside, but it felt like winter inside. This was a frozen house. A frozen place for her frozen heart.

She headed downstairs, her steps slow because of the heavy sadness inside her. She'd never loved Peter, but she'd followed her parents' orders and had married him. Now her parents were dead and her son was in prison. Her two daughters were married to men who worked under Peter. The girls were loyal to their father. They had to be for the sake of their husbands and their own daughters.

She was alone. Unloved. She had money and jewels and nothing else.

It wasn't right. It wasn't fair. It wasn't her fault.

For many years, she'd wondered if Peter would end their marriage. Now she could finally feel it coming.

If she could bring the baby back—the baby that had their son's blood running through his veins—that might be a game changer.

Only, how could she do this? How could she…

A thought came to her. So simple.

She turned, went back upstairs, sat down at her desk, opened her phone, and found her daughter-in-law's cell phone number. It rang once, then there was a click, and a message that the phone was not in service.

She set down the phone slowly. Now what?

After all these years, and after all the people she knew, she had no one to ask. No one to advise her. No true friends.

Looking around her room with the high ceilings and the gleaming desk and chair and bookshelves made of wood that came from Australia, she wondered if this was what hell looked like. The sun was lowering, and she glanced out the windows at the ocean. She realized that she'd rarely swum in the ocean. She had swum in their own pool instead. A place where there were no bugs and no sand.

The house phone rang. She glanced and saw it was her chef and it was nearly noon. Automatically, she reached for the phone and told him she'd be down in twenty minutes. And, no, Mr. Peter would not be dining tonight.

She hung up and sat still for a minute. Then she started to stand and then sat down again. Not yet. She had one more chance.

She opened her laptop, stared at it for a long moment, then typed in her daughter-in-law's email address. It might be possible that Polina hadn't deleted her email account.

For the subject line, she typed one word, all caps: *HELP.*

Then she sucked in a deep breath, positioned her fingers on the keyboard, and the words poured out from her soul.

My dear Polina,

You don't want the baby, but I do. My life is empty. I want to hold the baby in my arms.

Please. If you know anything, please tell me.

I promise on the baby's soul that I won't tell Peter.

I even promise that I won't tell Leo.

As much as I love my son, I can see what kind of person he is. I tried my best to raise him right, but everything I did to lift him up, Peter tore down. In Leo's eyes, Peter was the exciting parent. I was the strict parent. The non-fun parent.

You've walked away from Leo, and though he's my son, I can't blame you. In fact, I admire you for it. My marriage is a cold and stale thing. Peter and I haven't loved each other in a long time. To be honest, I don't think we ever loved each other. I'm going to imitate you and leave. My only reservation is that I don't want to walk away alone.

If you know anything about the baby's whereabouts, anything at all, even a clue, please, please tell me.

She paused. Should she offer to pay? Or would Polina feel insulted?

She sat a moment, then typed again.

Obviously, I can pay you for any information. I don't want to insult you, but if you need or want money, just say the amount. We can work out a way for me to send it to you. If you feel insulted, please pretend I never mentioned it.

I know I was a terrible mother-in-law, but I was terrible because I hated my life. I hated it that no one loved me. I didn't love myself.

Everyone needs to be loved by someone.

She stopped. Reread the last six paragraphs, then deleted the last three sentences.

Whatever you decide, I will understand and honor.

Best wishes on your new life. May it be filled with joy and laughter.

Olga

Sitting back, she read it over, then clicked on *send*. As she did, she wondered if Peter knew where the baby was. Of course, he must have tried to find the baby. He wouldn't have told her, because he was planning on divorcing her. Grandson or not, he probably would still try to impregnate his latest and very young girlfriend. Perhaps she was pregnant already, but she suspected that if it were true, a half dozen of the other wives would have told her.

The thoughts didn't make her angry. She didn't know if they were true. And if they were, it wasn't anything she could change.

She made up her mind. She would wait to see if Polina would contact her. If not … well, she wasn't sure what she would do, but perhaps it would be wise to start packing.

31

Another move. Susan glanced around Blake's kitchen. Her life had changed once again, though this change only required her and Hayley to carry her clothes to Blake's house next door while Wes and Blake carried Wes's clothes to the ranch home. A switch that at least five neighbors witnessed as they suddenly felt the need to stand on their lawns and the sidewalk to stare at them.

She suspected that a few more were peeking out of their windows.

"Should we charge our neighbors for entertainment?" Susan asked Blake in his bedroom in the back of the house. Wes had used the smaller bedroom—his choice—but she picked the bigger room because it had a bigger closet. She had a few more clothes than he did.

Blake laughed. "You don't know how cheap they are yet. To get any money out of them, you'd have to throw in a strip show."

She jabbed his ribs with her elbow. "I'm saving my strip shows for you."

He laughed. "Ditto. And since this is my house, you won't mind if I come for a stay-over once in a while."

"I think you should do that." She smiled at him. "You know, to protect me."

"I'm *very* good at protecting."

She laughed low in her throat. "Yes. Very."

"And I left a few clothes here, so I may as well stay."

She nodded and turned to hang her clothes in the closet, a smile building inside her, getting bigger by the minute.

Hi, Olga,

I hope this isn't a trap, but just in case, as soon as I send this, I'm deleting my account. Here's what I found out about myself since I left Miami.

It's only been a day, but I'm already carefree. I haven't reached "'happy," but I am feeling much better, as if "happy" isn't far away.

I like myself now. I had plans to steal Leo's baby away from the baby's mother, but I took off instead. If I'd done what I'd planned, I don't think I would be happy. How could I feel good if I knew I'd stolen another woman's baby?

Just a few weeks ago, I wouldn't have suspected that you had a conscience —but just a few weeks ago, you wouldn't have emailed me for advice. So my advice is this: LEAVE PETER. *You want my opinion of him? Well, whether you want it or not, I'm giving it. It's just four letters: JERK.*

To be honest, I could use other words, like MEAN and HEARTLESS. In any case, don't repeat any of this to him. Just find a good lawyer and get the hell out of that house you're rambling around in. (Sorry if you love your house, but it's half the size of a huge hotel. Do you really need that many rooms?)

Now I'm insulting you. *Normally, I'd give an email like this time to cool off, but there's no time for cooling off. So, here are my thoughts:*

First, *the divorce. I would have gotten one, but—I'm sorry to say this—I feared that Leo would have me killed. He's already blaming me for his choices.*

I would have loved *to have a baby, but I had still hoped to get pregnant. He was the one who refused to wait. The one who moved out of the house into the penthouse. The one who decided he needed a child right away. The one who searched for a woman who looked like me to be the baby's mama.*

I told *him it was wrong. It was insane. I finally agreed because he left me no other choice. He was going to do it with my permission or without. And now he's blaming me. Saying it's my fault and he wants to kill me.*

Once again I'm *sorry to say this, but your son isn't mentally healthy right now. (To say the least!)*

Of course, *since Leo's in prison, he wouldn't be able to kill me himself. But we both know he could pay someone else to do the job. I believe that if I'd stayed, it would have happened soon.*

So, here's my advice:

** Is there a place you've always wanted to visit? Then go. Do it. Travel around the world if you'd like. Or go to that one wonderful place and stay for a while.*

** Get a dog or a puppy. Or two dogs or puppies. Double the fun!*

** If you don't like dogs, get a cat. Or two cats.*

** Read books.*

** Get a hobby. Walk. Bird watch. (The dogs will walk with you.) Exercise. Swim. Play tennis. Take yoga classes. Join a book club. Knit. Sew. Crochet. Plant gardens. Learn how to brew beer. Paint. Knit. Crochet. Meditate. Bicycle. Rock climb. Keep bees. Go to Vegas and watch the Blue Man Group.*

** Look up old boyfriends. If they're healthy, ask them out for a date. If they aren't, join a dance club. Maybe you'll find a partner.*

You get the idea. And every night, when you go to bed, get on your knees and thank God that you're no longer married to Peter.

Or—if you want to stay in your house—you could kill Peter, hide the weapon, then say it was someone else. A masked man seems to work. Who could prove it wasn't?

Whatever you decide, I wish you the best. (And when you're done reading this, please delete.)

P

32

THE SUN WAS STILL HIGH IN THE SKY WHEN THE TWO men, wearing canvas slacks and short-sleeve shirts—casual business attire—drove the rental car out of the Green Bay-Austin-Straubel Airport parking lot.

"Where we going to eat?" the passenger asked. Andy was in his mid-thirties. He had a belly that, if he were a woman, people would guess he was three months pregnant. He was proud, though, of his thick black hair and his long fingers. Andy liked to say, "Long fingers mean a long schlong."

Paul, the driver, was in his mid-fifties. Old enough to be Andy's father, but they looked nothing alike. Paul was taller and thinner. He also liked to think he was smarter.

"We should shop for the baby stuff first," Paul said.

"I'm hungry."

"You're always hungry. We need to get the baby shit now, before we drive out there."

"Hey, how do you think the boss found the address?" Andy asked. "The Feds are usually pretty good at keeping the information to themselves."

"No one told me this," Paul said, "but it's my guess that it's Russian hackers."

"Yeah, we still got that Russian connection." Andy sighed. "I wish I knew how to hack. I don't know what the hell we're gonna do with a baby."

"The usual. You've got two kids. How old are they? One year and three years?"

"Yeah, something like that. But you think I do any of that shit?"

"No, I don't think you do much at all," Paul said, and was pleased when Andy glared at him. Paul had gotten stuck with this moron because the boss thought that, with two rugrats, Andy would know what the hell to do with a baby.

Paul would be happy when this was over with. He didn't have a good feeling about it. He'd done a lot of things that he was going to hell for, but stealing a baby was going to be the worst.

"I hope we don't have to kill the mom," he said.

"Tell you what," Andy said. "You take care of the baby, I'll kill the mom."

Paul tightened his grip on the steering wheel, and he kept driving. For a long time, he'd been thinking of getting out of the business. It was like stepping in quicksand. The quicksand never let go, but he wanted to give it a shot.

His second wife had left him two months ago, saying he was an idiot. Like she was a flippin' genius. His son from his first wife was in the army. Stationed in Alaska. After living in Miami for the last forty years, Paul didn't want to go to a place where it was so cold. But—"

"There's a Walmart." Andy pointed. "Next exit."

Paul hit the turn signal. Back to business. Shopping for a baby. He'd didn't mind the shopping part, but taking a baby from a mother... This was not going to be fun. Not at all.

Hayley stood in the middle of the living room. The place looked like a scene from a sitcom with her lover, her mother and her mother's lover—who was also the uncle of Hayley's lover—in the room. Then there was the tall, slender woman standing next to a handsome Irish wolfhound that was as tall as a small pony. The dog was bending his head to sniff Spock, who sniffed him back.

Lauren Donahue, the wolfhound's owner, was the mother of the three-month-old boy in the playpen with Finn, though she looked too put together to be the mother of a toddler. Hayley sighed. Some women just had that knack.

The two boys seemed to like each other, their happy gurgles catching Hayley's attention. Like Finn, Eric had red hair, only his was auburn where Finn's was red-gold. Though Finn was a couple months older, Eric was almost the same size as him.

The babysitter, an animated fourteen-year-old, was Adam Donahue's daughter and Lauren's stepdaughter. Hayley knew that Tori's mom had tragically died years ago, but she didn't remember how or when it happened. It was hard to keep up with everyone's background. What Hayley knew for sure was that the good-looking boy who was making the daughter laugh now—*Josh,* that was his name—was living with the Donahues but wasn't related.

Later, she would ask her mom why he lived with the Donahues. Susan might know. Hayley doubted if Wes knew or even wanted to know.

She groaned, and Wes put his hand on her back. She looked up at him.

"Something wrong?" he asked.

"I just realized," she said, her voice low, "that I'm getting to be as much of a gossip as anyone else in this town."

"Yeah? You know why?" Without waiting for her answer, he said, "You're starting to care. If you don't care, you don't want to know."

"What about you?" she asked. "When did you start caring?"

He smiled, his eyes bright, and he leaned closer to her ear. "The same day I looked out my window and saw a naked woman giving me the finger."

She sputtered with laughter. Her face warming, she turned in time to see that, except for the babies, everyone was watching them with goofy grins. *Embarrassing*. Hoping her face wasn't too pink, she turned to Lauren.

"Thanks for bringing your baby and the sitters here. We could have gone to your place."

"This worked out better," Lauren said. "We cleaned the carpet today, and the fumes aren't good for Tori."

"I'm okay!" Tori said.

"You were coughing." Her father gave her a stern look. "Besides, if it's bad for you, it's bad for the baby."

"And me." The boy tapped his breastbone and fake-coughed. "You know how sensitive I am."

"Jerk." Tori jabbed his arm with her elbow, and he laughed.

So did all the men.

Lauren rolled her eyes, and Susan chuckled. Hayley grinned. She felt normal today. Happy. As if the sun were shining inside of her.

"Let's go." Wes hugged her to his side, then loosened his grip. "Finn will be fine with his new friend. And Spock will watch over the babies, too. Finn loves Spock."

"The giant dog will guard them, too," Susan said.

"Tori and Josh, too." Adam beamed proudly at his daughter.

She grinned back at him. Hayley sighed. Lauren's husband with golden-brown hair and blue eyes was not bad to look at. She turned to Wes. Neither was he.

"Call if you need us," Wes said to the teens.

Hayley nodded. That should have been her line, but she felt fine leaving Finn with two babysitters and two dogs. They wouldn't be gone long. Probably three hours at the most. The resort where they were dining was only a few miles away. It was by the bay, so maybe they would take a walk after they ate.

And this was more than a friendly dinner. In addition to Adam's landscaping, snowplowing, plus handyman business, Adam made beautiful tables and benches. Blake and Wes were giving him room in their Art Mart space.

As a bonus, Adam's daughter was babysitting and Finn would play with another baby close to his age. Hayley had checked reviews for the restaurant on the Internet. It had a four-point-eight star rating. For a few hours, she would eat fine food and talk to adults—and be baby free.

She and her mother were making new friends, and even Spock was finding a new doggy friend.

Wes's hand settled on her shoulder. A warm feeling. As if she belonged to him, and he belonged to her. The warm feeling grew bigger. Brighter. She realized that since she'd left Miami, there had always been a small ball of fear inside her. The certainty that somehow Leo or his Mafia family would find her.

Finally, that fear was gone. Dissolved like sugar in a pan of boiling water.

Wes murmured, "You're quiet. What are you thinking?"

"I'm thinking this is going to be a great evening." She beamed at him. Maybe later she would tell him what she was really thinking. That tonight wasn't a happy ending for her.

It was a happy beginning.

33

IT WAS GETTING DARK OUTSIDE. OLGA CLOSED THE LAST suitcase. She was taking three big suitcases, two medium-sized suitcases, a couple of overhead suitcases, and three totes with her. All of them filled with stuff. She'd been packing for hours, deciding what to take and what to leave. She was sure that Polina had driven away from her place with much less than she did, but Polina was younger and freer.

Besides, Olga doubted that Peter would chase after her. He wouldn't consider her worth the manpower. And if anything did happen to her, someone might talk, and she was fairly certain that it would get to Leo. He wouldn't be happy if his father killed her.

As she straightened, her cell phone rang. She hesitated, then grabbed the phone from her dresser. The phone rang again. The Caller ID said *Unknown*. She frowned. The phone rang once more, and she hit the talk button. "Polina? Is that you?"

"Yes! I'm so glad I didn't toss my laptop yet. I wanted to make sure I got rid of it properly in case some computer wizard could trace—" Her words stopped, and Olga heard the hiss of her inhale. "Never mind. None of that matters. I received a message from the marshal. She didn't use her name, but it's the one that I made the deal with."

"The mother of the boy who needed a transplant?" Olga asked. Peter didn't usually share his dealings with her, but this was different. This had been about her grandson.

"That's the one," Polina said. "She'd received a phone call from a man who said he was speaking for me. He said I wanted the address of the place where the baby's living."

Olga's legs weakened. "She *gave* it to him?"

"She thought I'd changed my mind. She only called me after they hung up, just to make sure it was okay. Apparently, there was an article in the newspaper about the transplant. It mentioned that the boy's mother was a US Marshal. It's possible that Peter or one of his men saw it and connected the dots." Polina's voice rose. "There's nothing I can do about it. I feel awful. I feel—"

"Peter's men are going after Leo's son," Olga said, interrupting Polina. "That must be what happened. The address. Did she give you an address?"

"No. I didn't ask."

Olga slumped and closed her eyes. Since Peter hadn't mentioned it to her, he didn't plan to include her in the child's raising. And hadn't her family done enough harm to the mother of her grandchild? As much as she wanted the baby, she couldn't allow him to do this to the mother.

She had to do something. Even if she had to call the US Marshals Service herself and tell them to warn her grandson's mother.

"The marshal gave me the mother's phone number, too," Polina said. "I scribbled it down. Will that help?"

"Yes!" Olga's head snapped up. "Give it to me. I'll call and warn her."

"Are you sure—"

"I'm not sure of anything."

Polina's laugh was strangled. Then she told her the numbers.

Olga's mind felt numb as she took down the numbers, asking Polina to repeat them.

"Call me when it's taken care of," Polina said. "I won't destroy this phone until I hear from you."

"I will." She hung up and took a deep breath.

Then she tapped the numbers into her phone.

THEY HAD A CORNER TABLE, with a window view of Lake Michigan. The main meal was done, and Hayley felt like she was stuffed as a Thanksgiving turkey. She had turned down dessert, though she'd really wanted the lemon cream pie that Wes was eating.

The resort owner, a hunky guy with dark hair and an olive-skinned complexion, stopped and talked to the guys about fishing. He talked to Lauren for a moment, too. When he left, Wes said there was a story about him and his wife. He'd tell her later.

Lauren, who overheard, said everyone in Trouble Bay had a story. She and her husband grinned at each other, as if they were thinking of their own story.

Hayley's cell phone rang. She grabbed it, thinking it might be the babysitter. Looking at the caller ID, she saw a Miami area code and no name.

"Is everything all right?" Lauren asked.

She didn't reply. Not sure if she should answer.

It rang again. Making up her mind, she clicked and said, "Hello."

"Who is it?" Wes asked.

She held up her hand to silence him.

"This is..." The woman on the other end paused. "I don't know how to tell you this. I'm talking on a disposable phone, and I won't give you my name. But someone is coming to steal your baby."

Hayley sucked in her breath.

"I don't know when they'll be there," the woman continued. "I don't know if they're there already. I'm just telling you that it's going to happen, and it will happen soon. I have to go now. Take care of the baby."

There was silence. Whoever it was had hung up.

Hayley turned to Wes, her heart thumping. "We have to go home now. Fast."

"What is it?" he and Susan asked at the same time.

Hayley stood, shoving the cell phone in the side pocket of her navy blue palazzo pants. "A woman. She wouldn't give me her name, but she said someone is coming to steal the baby. We have to go now."

Everyone stood, but she didn't wait for them. She already turned and was running, not caring that she could feel the stares of the other diners. Then she remembered Wes's prosthetic, and she slowed, only to realize he was by her side. Thank God, because tears were blurring her eyes.

Finn. Her baby.

They zipped out of the restaurant. They hadn't paid, and she didn't care. Someone would pay. Someone would explain.

"We'll be there in five minutes," Wes said.

She heard hurrying footsteps behind them. A woman was saying something, her voice pitched high, but Hayley didn't look back. She was only looking forward, her heart in her throat.

34

Wes kept up with the others, grateful that he exercised every day. They'd come here in Blake's car, so he and Hayley jumped in the back, while Blake and Susan sat in the front. Two by two, Wes thought, as he reached for Hayley's hand. She gripped his as if she were hanging on for life. He didn't complain. He held on tight to hers, too.

He spotted Lauren and Adam jumping into their Jeep parked next to Blake's car.

In the front seat, Susan put her cell phone to her ear. "Come on," she said, her voice low. "Answer the phone. Please answer."

They all remained silent as Blake backed up his car, then turned toward the parking lot exit. Another car was turning in to the parking lot, and Blake drove slowly when Wes knew he wanted to roar out of here.

"Why aren't they answering?" Susan looked at Blake. "I double-checked to make sure I pressed Tori's phone number, and I did. You think she gave me the wrong number?"

Blake turned the car onto Bay Shore Drive, then drove to the road that took them into town. Tourist season had already started, and the roads were congested. Blake had to drive slowly again.

Wes was breathing too fast. Everyone was frustrated. Hayley wasn't saying a word, but her tight grip on his hand tightened more, her nails digging into the back of his hand.

"Maybe it's something simple," Blake said. "Maybe the kids are making out in the room away from the babies."

"I hope that's it," Susan said.

Wes could tell by the quaver in her voice she didn't believe it. As for him... He needed to focus. This was about the baby. *Both* babies right now. And the two teens, whether they were making out or shaking in their sneakers.

Or it could be something simple. They could be watching TV, the volume too loud to hear the phone ringing. Or they could be sitting on the front stoop as the babies napped, leaving their phone in the house.

Or one of them could be in the bathroom. Or they could both be using a bathroom. Unlikely, but there were two bathrooms in the house.

It could be *anything*.

But *anything* might be bad news.

"Spock's with the babies." He glanced at Hayley, who was sitting too still and too stiff, staring straight ahead. "You know he'll protect them. The babies and the teens."

"Finn will be okay," Blake said. "Don't worry."

Wes felt Hayley's worry and fear that no words could take away. He looked ahead again and mentally urged the traffic to move faster.

She had to see for herself that they were okay.

And so did he.

"WE DON'T WANT to kill you," Paul said, thinking, *Jesus. Kids.*

Two of them. And dogs. Big dogs. One giant-sized. The other one, the black lab, was growling at them. And the babies... There wasn't just one baby, there were two, and they both had red hair.

The teenaged boy, who looked like he was packing a few muscles, was eyeing Andy. Probably thinking he could take him. He was probably right, too. Andy was sweating like ... well, like a guy who could lose forty pounds. Or a guy who was scared.

Fuck. Fuck. Fuck. Fuck.

Though that should've reassured Paul. If Andy was scared, it meant he had some brains. Because he sure the fuck should be scared.

The black lab pushed up to a standing position in front of the playpen. The hair along its spine stuck straight up.

"Is that dog going to attack us?" Andy's voice pitched high like a girl's.

The cell phone that belonged to the one of the kids rang again.

Andy jumped. "I'm gonna throw the fuckin' thing in the toilet."

Paul shot him a look that should've shut him up, but Andy was busy glaring at everyone but him. For an instant, Paul wished the kid would sock Andy.

What a fuckup. This whole thing was so wrong. The black lab was growling low in his throat. His gaze was on Andy, at least, and not him.

But the big guy, the Irish wolfhound, wasn't taking his eyes off of Paul. Paul had a friend who had a dog like that. The dog looked calm but smart. Smart enough that the dog knew he was the guy who called the shots, not Andy.

Shit. Why were both babies redheads? Why were they both male?

"Just tell us which baby belongs to the lady who lives here," Paul said. "We won't touch the other one. If you don't tell us, we'll have to take both of them."

The girl's chin rose. Her mouth twisted in a sneer, and her gaze was scathing. She reminded Paul of his daughter when she'd been that age.

Oh, shit, oh, shit, oh, shit. The kid knew what they looked like. Both kids did.

He started to sweat. The only way to make sure they had the right baby would be to grab both babies and get the hell out of there.

If the dogs tried to attack them, they'd have to shoot them.

Oh, shit, oh, shit, oh, shit.

A million things could go wrong. Maybe he'd been doing this too long, but he wasn't ready to kill teenagers. And he sure the hell wasn't going to kill babies.

He was getting too damn old for this.

He dropped his right arm, the gun barrel aimed at the floor.

"What the fuck are you doing?" Andy asked.

Paul looked at him over his shoulder. "The sane thing," he said, then he turned away and started walking away.

"Why, you bast—"

There were fast sounds of dog feet hitting the carpet. Andy yelped, a dog barked. The other dog didn't say anything. Paul suspected the bigger dog had his teeth clamped onto Andy's arm. Instead of looking back to check, Paul walked faster. Then he was running, his heart pounding.

Behind him, babies cried and Andy shouted. Then Paul was out the door, running faster. As he reached the rental car, he spotted a man and woman hurrying down the sidewalk, straight toward the house he'd just left.

Paul hopped into the car. By now, someone had probably called the cops.

He started the car and pressed down on the gas, grateful that he'd smeared mud on the license plates. He'd dump the car in the next town and rent another one.

Andy probably wouldn't sing his heart out to the cops, but he'd sure the fuck tell the boss that Paul had walked out.

And what could Paul say to the boss? That the girl reminded him of his daughter? If he did, he knew for sure that something bad would happen to Jennie, even if she was all grown up, starting a dental practice with her husband in a small town in Georgia.

He turned onto the main road that was crowded with cars, but someone let him in as another car with two couples recklessly whipped past him.

He drove toward Sturgeon Bay, knowing there was only one thing he could do. Once he got to Sturgeon Bay, he'd stop someplace and look up the nearest US Marshal's building. Their witness protection program was starting to sound like a good idea.

35

HAYLEY WAS THE FIRST ONE TO RACE INTO THE HOUSE, the others behind her. Inside, it was chaos. The babies were crying. The kids were talking, their voices excited. Two neighbors from across the street were talking loudly. Spock was barking. A low, growling sound was coming from the Irish wolfhound lying on top of a man with thick hair.

"Get this giant fuckin' dog off me!" the man shouted.

Hayley ran past the kids, the dogs, the man, her gaze focused on the two babies in the playpen. Reaching the playpen, she bent, then lifted her wailing son, hugging him against her chest and rubbing his back.

Next to her, Lauren did the same thing with her crying son.

Behind her, Blake was asking what happened. Susan asked at the same time, and so did Adam. Everyone talked at once.

The babies cried louder.

Hayley turned to Lauren, who was trying to shush her son. "Should we go in my bedroom or the backyard?"

Lauren nodded, then crooned to her son.

As they walked outside, the sheriff's car rolled up. A deputy jumped out of the passenger side. "What happened?" he called out.

"Go in the house," Lauren yelled back at him.

The other officer ran past him, but the first stayed. "You shouldn't leave.

"We'll be in the backyard," Lauren said. "It's too noisy for the babies in there."

As if on cue, Lauren's baby howled. The deputy winced. "I got one of those at home, too. Just don't go anywhere."

Then he hurried to the front door. Hayley noticed people walking her way.

"Let's go now," she called out to Lauren. "Before we're mobbed."

Lauren walked to the backyard with her. There were two plastic chairs, and they sat down and murmured soothingly to their babies. Calming them. Massaging their backs until they both settled, safe now in their mothers' arms.

Hayley heard the others talking in the front yard—just their voices, too far away to hear their words, especially when two or more spoke at the same time. The deputies' voices were stern. Talking with the authority of their badges.

Finally, the voices separated, one at a time. The kids first. She still couldn't hear what they were saying. Later, she would find out the details.

"The moon is shining," she said. "The kids are okay."

Lauren laughed shakily. "Thank the lord."

"And the dogs."

"And whoever it was who called you."

"I almost forgot." Still holding Finn with her left hand, she dug her right hand into her palazzo pants pocket and pulled out her cell phone. A minute later, she was talking to the same woman who'd warned her, telling her that they and the babies were okay. She started to tell more, but the woman cut her off.

"That's all I need to know," she said. "I'm glad for you. Now, I'm going to get rid of the cell phone so no one will ever find it."

Before Hayley could tell her how to discard the phone, the woman said, "Good-bye."

Hayley listened to dead air.

"Who was that?" Lauren asked.

"She wouldn't tell me her name." Hayley slid the phone back in her pocket. "But I think she's my hero."

36

HAYLEY FELT NUMB AS THE SKY TURNED A DARK GRAY, the moon a sliver. The deputies asked them different versions of the same questions too many times. Finally, they said they might have more questions tomorrow, and they left. A few minutes later, Lauren and Adam, the two teens, their baby, and their giant dog drove away, too. Blake, Wes, Hayley, and Susan moved the baby's playpen and bassinet and clothes to Wes's place. Just in case someone came back.

Hayley didn't say much at all. Her worst fears had come true.

She had to keep reminding herself that they were okay. No one had stolen Finn or the other baby. One of the bad guys was caught. The other had left because he couldn't stomach what they were doing. For that alone, Hayley hoped he would be okay.

Finn made a few noises, but he soon settled down, sleeping peacefully in the bassinet in Wes's old room.

"Susan and I are staying here tonight." Blake sat on the couch next to Susan.

Wes handed a bottle of beer to his uncle and Susan. "I'll get wine for you," he said to Hayley.

"Beer is fine." She held out her hand. She wasn't a big drinker, even before she breastfed, but a beer sounded good right now.

"I brought my gun." Susan held up her purse, then looked at Hayley. "You should finish the target shooting training and get a gun license."

Hayley shrugged. She would think about it. She sat on a recliner. "I wonder what will happen to the guy who walked away."

"He should go to prison," Wes said, sitting on the other recliner.

"I hope he gets put away," Susan said.

Hayley nodded. "I just hope no one else looks for us."

"After this disaster," Blake said, "I doubt whoever did this will try anything else."

"I doubt it, too," Wes said. "They had their shot, and they blew it."

"I suppose the marshals will move us somewhere else soon," Susan said.

Hayley stared at her, her breath catching in her lungs. Neither man spoke. Or moved. It seemed that all of them had frozen.

"I just thought of something." Susan's voice was bright. "We won't have to move somewhere else. It's so easy to fix this."

"What is this brilliant solution?" Blake asked.

"We changed our names once. We can change them again." She beamed at him.

Hayley frowned. "What about the people who live here? They'll know."

"Your mother's right," Blake said. "What happens in Trouble Bay stays in Trouble Bay."

"Really?" Hayley asked. "People love to talk. And look at the audience we had."

"A regular circus," Blake agreed. "Probably all the neighbors heard the idiot as he spilled his guts."

"He was really afraid of the Irish wolfhound." Susan giggled. "I *love* that dog."

They all smiled for a minute. For a minute everyone was at peace.

Wes broke the silence. "After this fiasco, I doubt the Mafia boss will send anyone else here. If anyone tries to steal Finn again, the police and the marshals would be all over the boss and anyone who knows him. He won't take the chance."

"I agree with my smart nephew." Blake turned to Susan on the couch, his knee knocking against her knee closest to him. "In any case, I have a better solution."

"I'm all ears." Susan smiled at him.

"Marry me. Take my last name."

Her mouth opened. No words came out for a moment.

Hayley winced. Her mother never wanted to get married. She'd told Hayley that a hundred times. She loved men, but—

"You said you're not good at marriage," Susan said.

"That's because I wasn't married to you."

"I'm not that special."

He smiled slowly. Watching him, Hayley melted a bit.

"You're right. You aren't *that* special. You're much more."

Susan stared at him as if she were transfixed. "I never wanted to be married before."

"You told me that you're not good at long-term relationships," he said. "I prefer long-term, but to save your life—and keep you from leaving—I'll settle for short-term. If you want to divorce me after a few years, I won't try to stop you."

There was silence in the room. Hayley could hear their four hearts thrumming, or maybe it was the plumbing. Or maybe it was the sky and the moon and the earth, but everything seemed more alive and more vibrant tonight as the seconds ticked by.

"For years I've said that I never wanted to settle for one man," her mother whispered, "but that's not it. Not really."

"What is it?" Blake asked, his eyes not leaving hers.

Watching them, Hayley breathed lightly, not wanting to miss a syllable.

"The men I were seeing stopped being fun after a while." Susan frowned. "Sometimes the change happened in a few weeks. Sometimes months. They changed. More interested in what was on TV or their friends or their football teams than being with me."

"Susan, I—"

She raised her hand, stopping him. "I'm not talking about forever dancing and partying with me, but just ... *listening* to me. *Laughing* with me. Just being my best friend."

"Is that it?" Blake smiled at her. "When we take our vows," he said in a low voice, "my vow to you will be to love you more than football or politics or fishing or anything that's on TV. Definitely more than other women."

She sniffed. "I was never worried about other women."

He laughed, and she beamed at him.

Hayley grasped Wes's hand, and he grasped hers back.

"I don't know if I can keep being fun as the years go by," Blake said, "but one thing I can promise is that I will keep on loving you. I'll engrave that on my wedding ring."

"You mean that?"

"With all my heart," he said, and then they kissed.

Hayley stood, and so did Wes. "We should go somewhere else," she said, her voice low.

Her mother laughed and stood. So did Blake, slinging his arm around Susan's shoulders. "You stay, Hayley," Susan said. "Blake and I will go to the other bedroom. Won't we?"

His laugh was wicked. Holding hands, they hurried down the hall, leaving Hayley and Wes in the living room.

37

HAYLEY SIPPED HER BEER, THEN SET THE BOTTLE ON THE side table next to the recliner. Looking up at Wes, she said, "I'm not worried about relocation."

"No?" He raised an eyebrow.

"I'm not moving. I think Blake's right. Just in case, I'll change my last name, but I don't have to do anything so dramatic as marry anyone."

"You don't, huh?"

She shrugged. "If anyone wants to find me, they'll probably think the marshals moved me to another state."

He stared at her, and she blinked, knowing her eyes were watering. Not crying, just watering. Emotional after everything that had happened tonight.

She sniffed, hoping he didn't think she was crying over him.

He pushed out of his recliner, then stepped over to her and held out his hand. "Come to the sofa with me. Before you make any decision, I have something to show you."

She opened her mouth to say she didn't need help, but he

leaned forward and took her hand. She allowed him to draw her up, pushing up with her other hand so she wouldn't pull him down on top of her. In silence, they walked around the coffee table to the couch. He still held her hand as they sat down.

"Are you all right?" he asked.

She nodded. "I'm happy for my mom."

"You look a little sad."

"Maybe I am, a little. It was a scary night. And there will be changes again. I don't like change. I don't want to move, not really."

"You fit into this town."

"I do. I feel good living here." She looked into his eyes. "I feel ... that this place is just right for me. I fit into the smallness. Since I've been here, so many parts of my life that had felt wrong for years just tumbled around to feeling good."

"And your mother is staying here."

She looked at him. "And so are you."

He smiled. Not just his mouth, but his eyes. "Am I a big part of the reason you'd like to stay?"

"Yes," she said, her voice husky. "Yes."

Smiling with his eyes and his mouth, he reached into his pants pocket. "I told you I have something for you."

Her heart pounded as she watched him pull his hand out from his pants pocket, holding a small velvet bag. He opened the bag and drew out a silver ring with a green stone.

She looked up, and his brown eyes blazed. "I got this a week ago," he said, "at the Art Mart. It's an emerald. I thought it suited you more than diamonds, but if you don't—"

"I love it, but—"

"I love *you*." He still held it in his hand. "The artist is from Sister Bay. If you don't like it, she said she'd take it back. You can pick out—"

"Stop." She pressed her fingers against his mouth, making sure his lips stopped moving before taking away her hand. "I *love* the ring. But I don't want you to ask me right now just because you feel you should."

"You're missing something."

"What?"

"I said I loved you. You didn't say it back."

She stared at him, then smiled slowly. "Of course I love you. How can I not? You're so—" Tears clogged her throat and filled her eyes. Happy tears. She shook her head.

"So wonderful?" He smiled slowly back at her. "Is that what you're trying to say?"

She laughed and cried at the same time. It took both of them to put the ring on her finger. Not because it didn't fit her perfectly, but because her hand kept shaking. Finally, she flung her arms around his shoulders. "Yes!" she said. "Yes, yes, yes, I'll marry you."

He laughed and kissed her, long and sweet.

A loud sigh came from Wes's other side. They pulled apart at the same time, and they both glanced down at Spock. The black lab was lying on the rug by Wes's feet, staring up at him with a question in his eyes.

"I think he's wondering if we're done yet," Hayley said.

"Sorry, Spock." Wes swung his gaze to her, his lips curving up. "We're not done. We're just beginning."

She smiled, then laughed.

"Let's go to bed," They both turned toward the hallway and walked to the bedroom. She was in front, and he was behind her. Behind him she could hear Spock's feet.

"The baby's in here," she whispered, stopping before they stepped inside and twisting to face Wes. "I suppose we could still make love with him here. Quietly."

His eyes smiled at her again. "You don't make quiet love."

She laughed and slapped her hand over her mouth to muffle the sound. "I'm already noisy."

"Sleeping is fine," he said. "We have a lifetime to make love. A lifetime together."

She beamed at him. Then, hand in hand, they walked into the bedroom, the baby inside, the dog behind them. A family already.

38

Six weeks later

The phone rang. It was early, but Hayley was up. Though it was her wedding day, Finn had woken her a few minutes after seven. She'd just finished feeding him and was cutting half a grapefruit on the kitchen counter while Finn played with the suction toy on the tray of his highchair.

Checking Caller ID, Hayley recognized the phone number of her assigned US Marshal. Her nerves tightened. She put the phone to her ear, wondering why Tracey was calling. They'd invited her to the wedding, but Tracey had sent her regrets and a nice card. No gift, because she and Wes had told everyone they didn't need anything but blessings and happy wishes.

"Tracey, is something wrong?"

"Hi, Hayley. I'm glad I didn't wake you. I have news. A lot has happened, and I'm calling before you read about it in the papers."

"What is it?"

"This actually happened a while ago, but no one noticed until lately."

"Noticed what?"

"Polina Vasnev, Leo Vaznev's wife, has disappeared."

"Really? I hope it's not because she's been ... you know. Whacked."

"No! At least, we don't think so. We believe that more than a month ago she left of her own accord."

Hayley stiffened. Was it Leo's wife who had called her to warn her about the two thugs who were going to kidnap Finn?

"Good for her," she said.

"I agree. In my opinion, she had a raw deal. The bigger news is that Leo's father, Peter Vasnev, died. Heart attack. Supposedly by natural causes. But who knows for sure? Anyway, the new mob boss is not a fan of Leo. When Leo finally gets out of prison, I doubt that he'll want him on his team."

"Interesting."

"It's not my case, but it's not classified. Consider it my wedding present to you. And that's not all. There's more."

"About Leo?"

"His mother. Apparently, she left her husband and was hiding from him. Now that he's dead, she's returning to Miami to sell the house. I've heard that she plans to move to Arizona. Maybe she likes the heat but can't take the humidity. I can't say that I blame her."

Hayley was glad she was sitting. "How will this affect us? Are my mother and I out of the program?"

"When I know something, I'll let you and Susan know." Tracey huffed. "Your whole life was changed by everything that happened, and now it might seem to be a waste, but—"

"Are you kidding?" Hayley's voice rose, and so did she, getting to her feet.

Her mom walked into the kitchen, her eyebrows up in a question. For this last day, Susan had insisted that Hayley and Wes sleep apart.

Hayley had thought it was hilarious, but both she and Wes had let her mother have her way.

"Just a minute. My mom is here." Hayley took the phone from her mouth, holding it to her chest. "It's Tracey. Leo's father died of a heart attack. Someone else has taken over the Russian mob, and now no one cares about Leo."

"What about our protection? We don't have to worry about it anymore, do we?"

"Tracey said—" She stopped and held out the phone to her mom. "Here. You talk to her. I'll put the phone on speaker mode."

Her mother remained standing, and so did Hayley as the two women greeted each other. After listening to Tracey's news, her mother said she was stunned. "Do they need us to remain in the witness program?" she asked.

"For now, you're still in the program," Tracey said. "It's possible Leo might have some pull in the organization. I doubt it, but we think it's best to keep you under the radar until we know for sure."

Susan thanked her, then handed the phone back to Hayley.

"The wedding is still on today?" Tracey asked.

"Yes!"

"And your mother? What about her guy?"

Hayley grinned at her mom, who was putting water into the coffeemaker. "They're letting us marry first."

Her mother grabbed the phone. "Only because Wes already had the ring," she said. She and Tracey talked for another minute, then hung up.

Hayley looked at her mom. "You might be able to go back to Miami soon. I'm staying in Trouble Bay, but you don't have to stay here. You don't have to marry Blake."

"I hate winters." Her mom grimaced. "I miss the warm weather. I miss the music scene in Miami. I miss the Cuban restaurants. I miss my friends. I even miss seeing your father once in a while, talking about you and listening to him telling me what to do with my money."

Hayley nodded, biting her lower lip.

"But if I left," Susan's voice softened, "I would miss my new business. I would miss my new man even more. I would miss my grandson. And I would miss my favorite creation. *You.*" She grinned. "I meant what I said to Blake. I *want* to marry him. He makes me happy."

There was a knock on the front door. "It's us!" Blake called through the screen door that they'd kept locked from the inside.

"Coming!" Susan headed to the front door.

Hayley followed her mother who was taking fast strides across the living room. As they neared the front door, Hayley could see the faces of her soon-to-be husband and her mother's lover. Susan unlocked the screen door, and Wes stepped in first, and Spock behind him. Blake stayed on the front stoop.

"I'll leave the soon-to-be bride and groom alone for a few minutes." Susan laughed and stepped outside into the sunshine and into the arms of her future husband.

Hayley grinned. Wes grinned back.

The baby in the kitchen cried out, "*Ock! Ock!*"

Hayley put her right hand over her breast, staring at Wes. "Did Finn say his first word? Spock's name?"

"I think he did." Wes gazed down at Spock and pointed at the kitchen. "Finn wants you. He's calling your name. What are you waiting for?"

"*Ock!*" Finn called. "*Ock!*"

Spock barked, then barreled down the hall and into the kitchen.

"My son is a genius," she said.

"My son now, too." He stepped closer and slid his arms around her, the small paper bag in his hand crinkling.

Happy tears warmed her eyes, and she grasped his upper arms.

He smelled like a mix of shaving cream and cinnamon. "You couldn't stay away from me, could you?"

"I missed you sleeping next to me last night." His voice was low. "I love you. I plan to make you happy. Starting with kisses and cinnamon rolls."

They kissed, then she loosened her grip and stepped back. "I have to let Finn out of the chair."

"We don't want him to fall." He held the paper bag up high. "My first wedding present to you."

She laughed. "Cinnamon rolls. Best wedding present ever. Next to you, of course."

He grinned. She remembered when they'd first seen each other. He'd stared at her breasts, and she'd given him the finger. She laughed.

"I'm a lucky guy." He walked down the hall with her. "You know what I think?"

The screen door slammed in the living room. The other pair of love birds returning. Hayley guessed they wanted to claim their share of cinnamon rolls, too.

She and Wes turned into the kitchen where Finn was hitting the tray of the high chair, saying, "Ock! Ock! Ock!"

Spock barked at him, a happy bark.

Hayley stopped and looked up at Wes. "What *do* you think?"

"Think about what?" her mom asked, striding into the kitchen, Blake following her.

"I think," Wes said slowly, glancing at everyone in the room—including Spock—with his gaze coming back to her, "that today is just the beginning of a wonderful life."

Love filled her. She suspected if she looked in the mirror she would see herself glowing with happiness.

There was silence for a moment, then they all grinned. As Hayley looked around, she saw that even Spock's mouth was opened in a smile, and Finn gurgled with laughter.

A memory came back to her of the night she'd gone to Leo's penthouse. The night she'd found out about his lies. That was the day she'd thought she was in a soap opera. Perhaps she had been then. Now she was in a fairy tale, and she didn't want it to end for a long, long time...

THANK YOU!

Thanks for reading *Do-Over Love & Murder*. I'm having so much fun writing this series, and I hope you're enjoying reading the books. ***Reviews are very much appreciated!*** This is my sixth Love & Murder book—not counting the Unforgettable Love & Murder short story that I'm giving away to new newsletter subscribers. (If you're already a subscriber who missed my notice, contact me.)

I'm working on a new series set in Arizona. It will have paranormal elements, and will also have the tone and the emotion that are in my Love & Murder books, along with a mix of mystery and danger. And pets, of course. I'm so looking forward to writing the first one.

Wishing you great reading and magic!

Edie Ramer

www.edieramer.com

ABOUT THE AUTHOR

A *USA Today* bestselling author, Edie Ramer is funnier on the page than in real life. She writes stories with heart, attitude, suspense, and sometimes humor. A lifelong Wisconsin resident, she lives in Arizona now with her husband and one very important cat. She's happy to be able to do what she loves nearly every day, and she loves hearing from readers.

Connect with Edie:

www.edieramer.com

OTHER TITLES BY EDIE RAMER

Books by Edie Ramer

Love & Murder series

Truth About Love & Murder, Book 1

Rules of Love & Murder, Book 2

A Love & Murder Christmas, Book 3

Raining Love & Murder, Book 4

Christmas Redemption, Book 5

Do-Over Love & Murder, Book 6

Rescued Hearts series

Hearts in Motion, Book 1

Christmas at Angel Lake, Book 2

Crazy Sexy Love, Book 3

Finding Awesome, Book 4

Miracle Interrupted series

Must Worship Cats. Book 1

Stardust Miracle, Book 2

Miracle Lane, Book 3

Miracle Pie, Book 4

Mo's Heart, Book 5

Miracle Interrupted Set (first 3 books)

Paranormal

Dragon Blues

Dragon Mama Blues (a novella)

Cattitude

The Fat Cat (a Cattitude short story)

Dead People

Dead People In Love (a Dead People short story)

Galaxy Girls

Mixing It Up, a Galaxy Girls novella